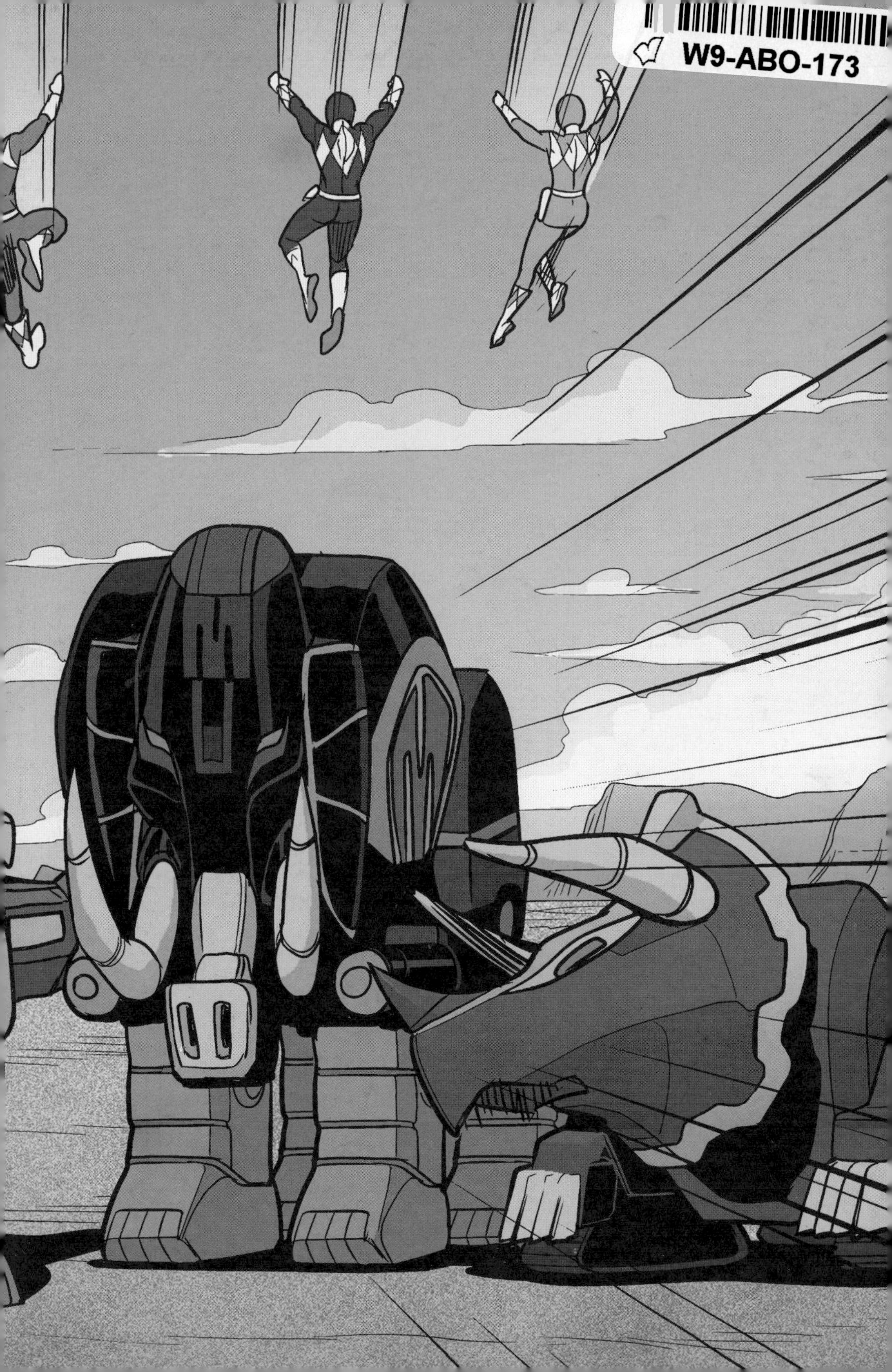

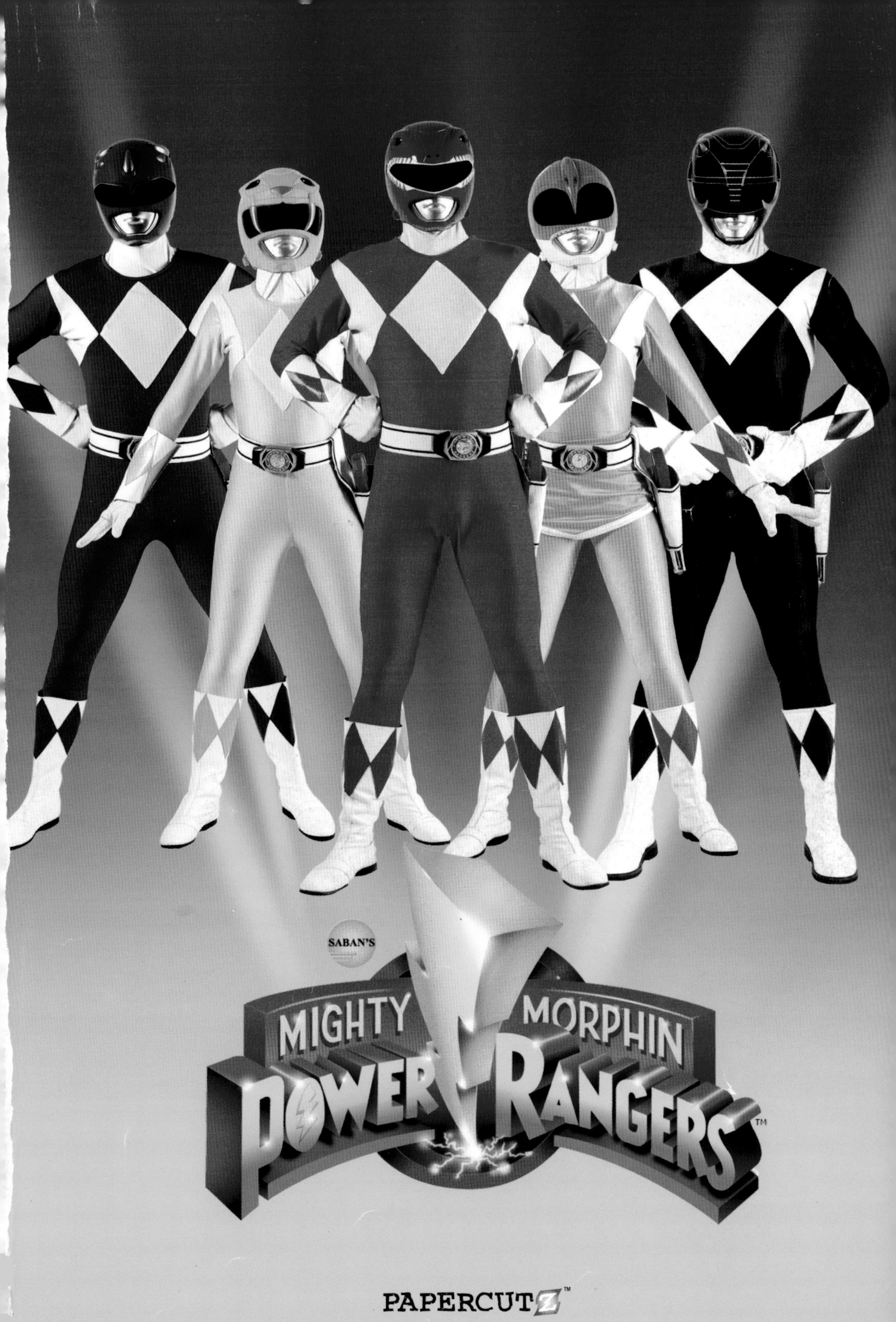

SABAN'S

MIGHTY MORPHIN

POWER RANGERS™

PAPERCUTZ™

SABAN'S POWER RANGERS

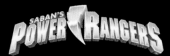

Graphic Novels by Stefan Petrucha and PH Marcondes, available from Papercutz

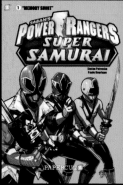

1 "MEMORY SHORT"
SABAN'S POWER RANGERS
SUPER SAMURAI
Stefan Petrucha
Paulo Henrique
PAPERCUTZ

Super Samurai #1

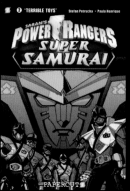

2 "TERRIBLE TOYS"
Stefan Petrucha • Paulo Henrique
SABAN'S POWER RANGERS
SUPER SAMURAI
PAPERCUTZ

Super Samurai #2

SABAN'S POWER RANGERS
MEGAFORCE
PAPERCUTZ

Megaforce #4

SABAN'S POWER RANGERS
MEGAFORCE
"GAME ON!"
PAPERCUTZ

Megaforce #3

RITA REPULSA'S
ATTITUDE ADJUSTMENT
Stefan Petrucha
PH Marcondes
MIGHTY MORPHIN
POWER RANGERS
THEY'RE BACK!
PAPERCUTZ

Mighty Morphin Power Rangers #1

POWER RANGERS graphic novels are available for $6.99 each in paperback, and $10.99 in hardcover except volume 4 and MIGHTY MORPHIN POWER RANGERS #1, $7.99pb/$11.99hc. Available at booksellers everywhere. You can also order online from papercutz.com. Or call 1-800-886-1223, Monday through Friday, 9 – 5 EST. MC, Visa, and AmEx accepted.

To order by mail, please add $4.00 for postage and handling for first book ordered, $1.00 for each additional book and make check payable to NBM Publishing. Send to: Papercutz, 160 Broadway, Suite 700, East Wing, New York, NY 10038.

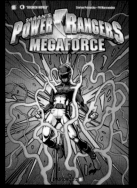

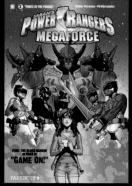

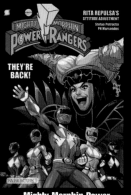

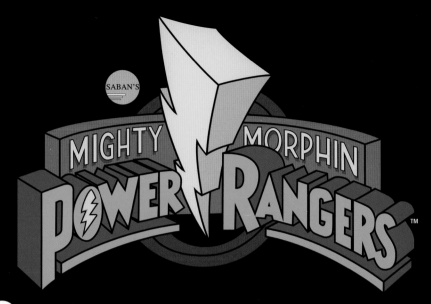

SABAN'S

MIGHTY MORPHIN POWER RANGERS™

1 "RITA REPULSA'S ATTITUDE ADJUSTMENT"

Stefan Petrucha – Writer
PH Marcondes – Artist
Laurie E. Smith– Colorist

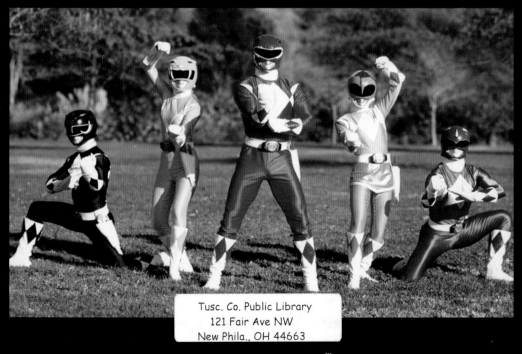

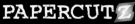

PAPERCUTZ™

MIGHTY MORPHIN POWER RANGERS #1
"Rita Repulsa's Attitude Adjustment"

STEFAN PETRUCHA – Writer
PH MARCONDES – Artist
LAURIE E. SMITH – Colorist
BRYAN SENKA – Letterer

UMESH PATEL (RANGER CREW) – Special Thanks
KAY OLIVER, MARY RAFFERTY, GREG SANTOS – Extra Special Thanks
BETH SCORZATO – Production Coordinator
MICHAEL PETRANEK – Editor
JIM SALICRUP
Editor-in-Chief

ISBN: 978-1-59707-696-8 paperback edition
ISBN: 978-1-59707-697-5 hardcover edition

Printed in China
April 2014 by New Era Printing LTD
Unit C, 8/F Worldwide Centre
123 Chung Tau Street, Hong Kong

Papercutz books may be purchased for business or promotional use. For information on bulk purchases please contact
Macmillan Corporate and Premium Sales Department at (800) 221-7945 x5442.

Distributed by Macmillan

First Printing

After 10,000 years of imprisonment, the evil sorceress Rita Repulsa and her loyal minions have been freed from their space dumpster, when astronauts on a routine mission accidentally opened it on the moon. Enraged, Rita decided to conquer the nearest planet-- Earth. But her arch nemesis, the heroic sage Zordon, has been patiently waiting for this day.

  With the assistance of his wisecracking robotic sidekick Alpha-5, Zordon recruits 5 "teenagers with attitude"-- Jason, Kimberly, Billy, Trini, and Zack-- to receive superpowers beyond their wildest dreams and defend the Earth as the Mighty Morphin Power Rangers. Aided by giant robotic vehicles modeled after dinosaurs called "Zords," the Power Rangers fight back the evil alien hordes of Rita Repulsa.

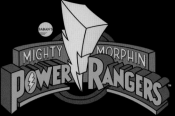

THE RED RANGER (JASON LEE SCOTT)

Jason is a black belt in karate and the leader of the Power Rangers. His martial arts are his passion and he spends much of his free time training, both learning new moves and perfecting old ones. When he's not training Jason is working on his schoolwork or hanging out with friends, like most other seventeen-year-old guys.

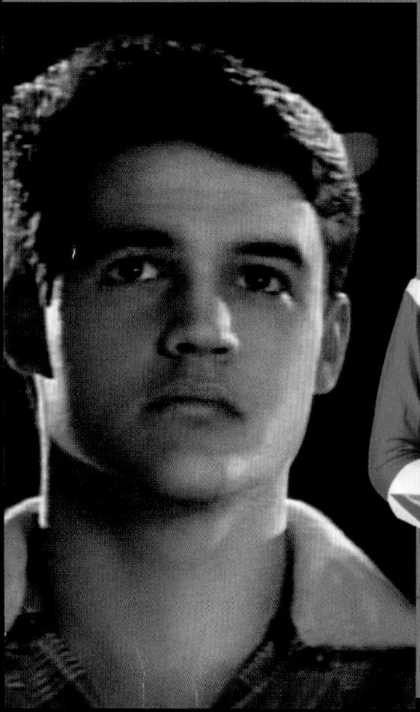

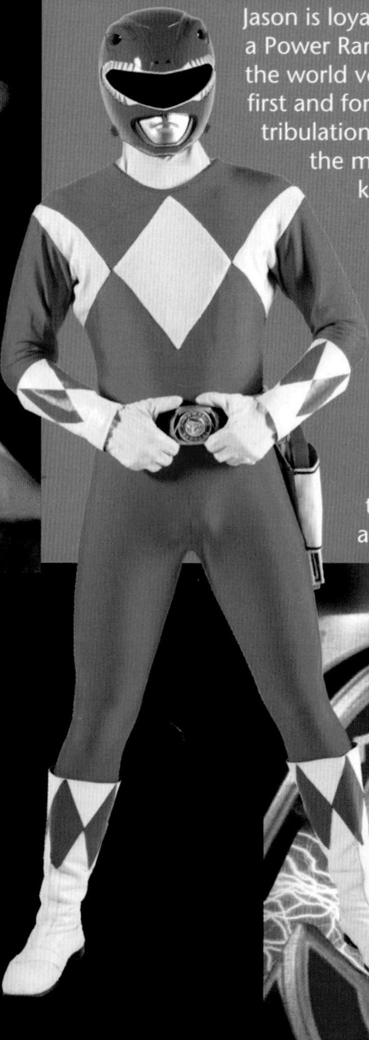

Jason is loyal and patriotic. He loves being a Power Ranger and takes his duty to save the world very seriously. But he's still a teen first and foremost, with all the trials and tribulations that entails. Jason isn't always the most outspoken guy, preferring to keep his feelings to himself, and letting his hands and feet do the talking while fighting with the Power Rangers. But even with his rough exterior, his sly smile can reveal the mischievous boy-next-door he is at heart.

Jason draws power from the Tyrannosaurus rex. His weapon is the Power Sword, and he pilots the Megazord when it is fully assembled.

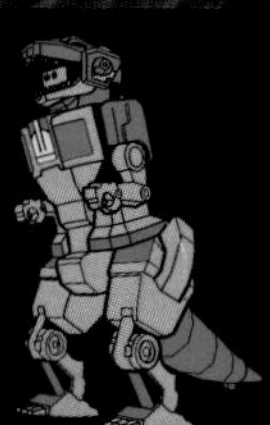

Weapon:
Power Sword

Zord:
Tyrannosaurus Dinozord

Notes:
Jason was a martial arts instructor at Ernie's Juice Bar and Gym

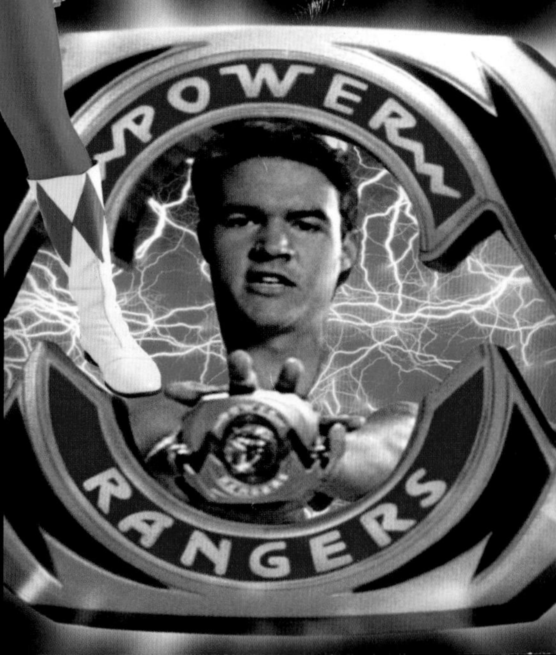
POWER
RANGERS

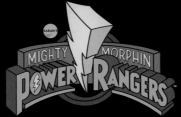

THE PINK RANGER (KIMBERLY HART)

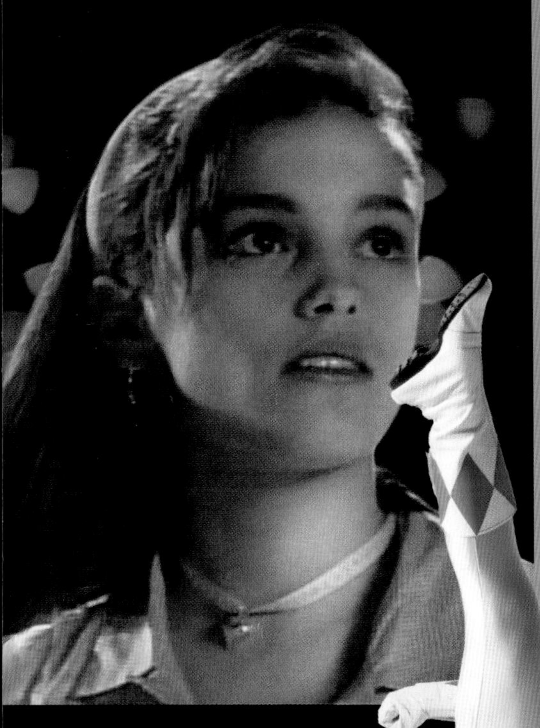

Kimberly is a bright and beautiful girl who loves shopping and gymnastics. She's the most popular girl at school and loves the attention of the limelight. But beneath her bubbly exterior she's fiercely independent and has always longed for adventure and danger. Kimberly is always upbeat with her friends, but she's got a wicked streak of sarcasm and one-liners that she saves for the bad guys.

Kimberly is also a champion gymnast, and she brings these skills to her work with the Power Rangers. She trains hard not just to compete, but also to be able to jump and flip her way out of almost any situation. With the Power Rangers, Kimberly draws power from the Pterodactyl and her weapon is the Power Bow.

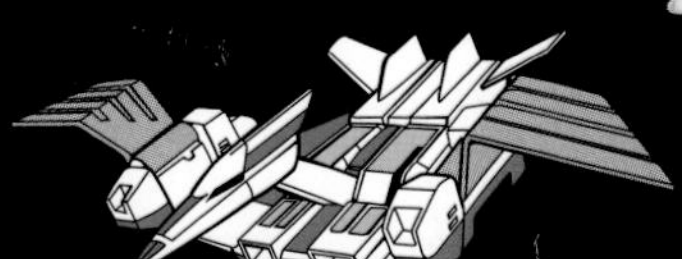

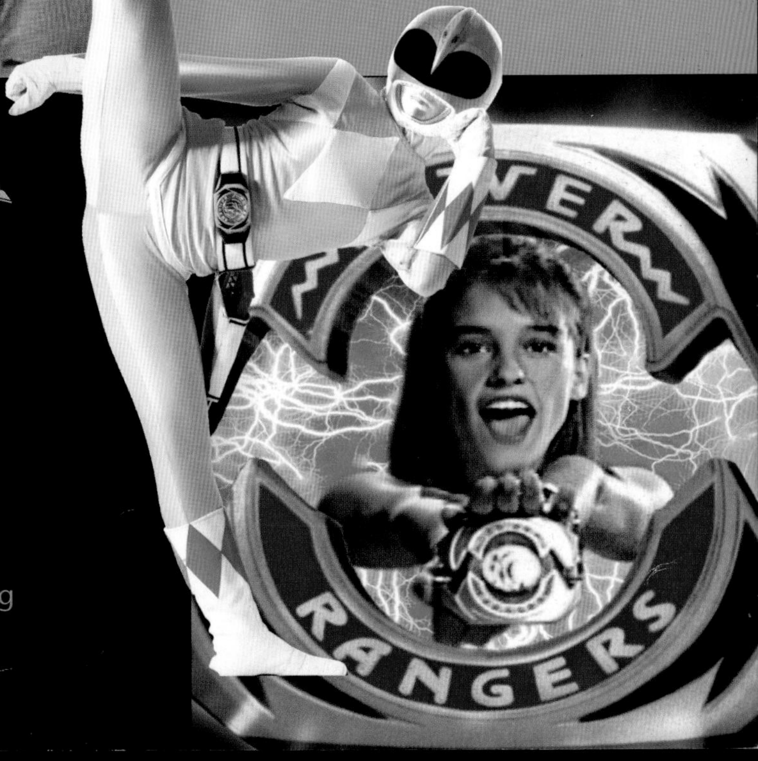
RANGERS

Weapon:
Power Bow

Zord:
Pterodactyl
Dinozord

Notes:
Local bully Skull has a big crush on her.

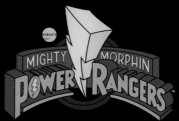

THE BLUE RANGER (BILLY CRANSTON)

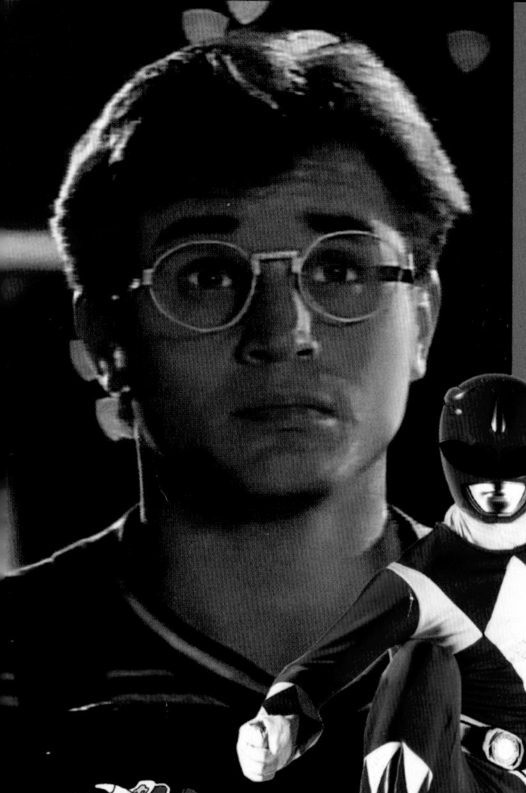

Billy is super-smart and this can sometimes get in the way of him communicating with other kids. But once they get to know him they realize that he's more than just a nerd. Billy is sweet and kind-hearted, on top of being a super-genius. He focuses all his energy on his academics and often talks in techno-speak, using complicated language that confuses most people. Lucky for him, Trini always seems to understand.

Billy always wants to know how everything works and is constantly studying the world around him. His greatest hobby is learning. In spite of his intelligence, Billy is usually shy and reserved, except for with his friends, the other Power Rangers. With them he feels like he can truly be himself.

As a Power Ranger, Billy draws power from the Triceratops and his weapon is the Power Lance.

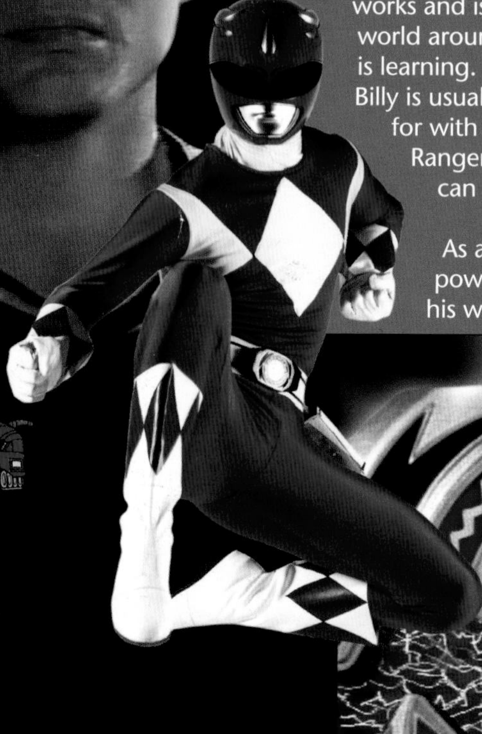

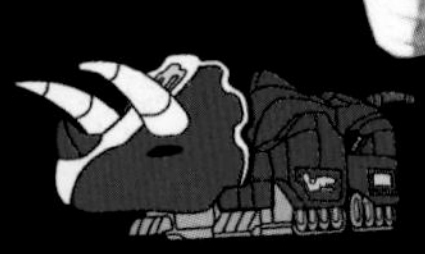

Weapon:
Power Lance

Zord:
Triceratops
Dinozord

Notes:
Billy built the Power Ranger communicators.

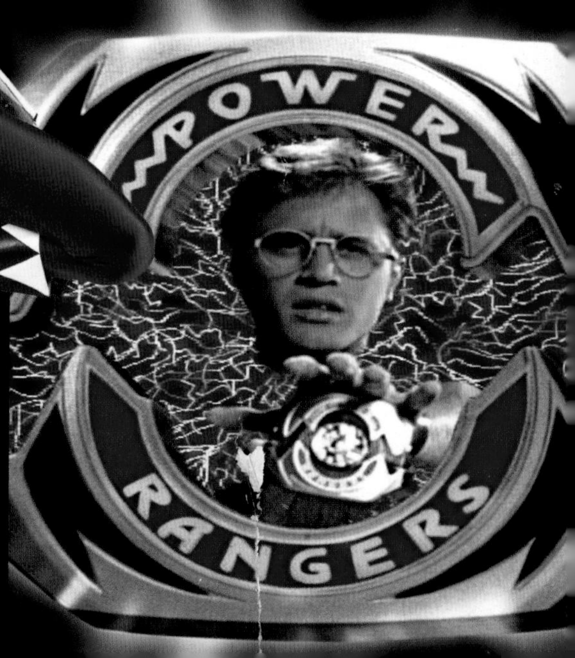
POWER
RANGERS

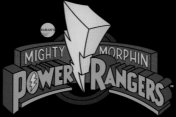

THE YELLOW RANGER (TRINI KWAN)

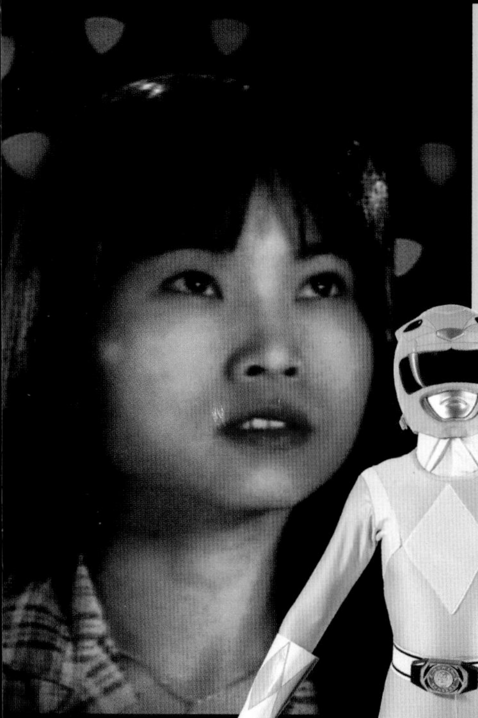

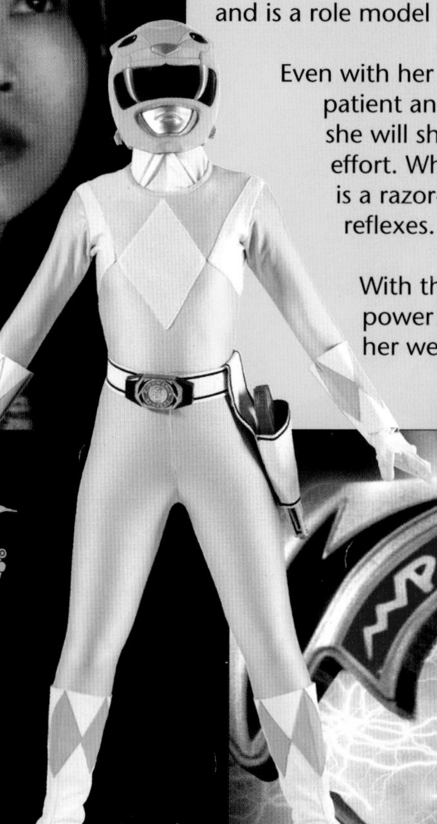

Trini has been described by Zordon himself as the one with "lightning hands and a peaceful soul." She is deeply dedicated to her martial arts practice, constantly working on both the spiritual and physical aspects of her karate. Trini is highly observant and highly intelligent, which makes her the only person who truly understands Billy. At school, Trini is active in lots of activities and causes and is a role model for other students.

Even with her extraordinary gifts, she is very patient and slow to anger. But, if pushed, she will shut down any threat with little effort. When her training takes over, she is a razor-sharp fighter with lightning reflexes.

With the Power Rangers, Trini draws power from the Sabertooth Tiger, and her weapon is the Power Daggers.

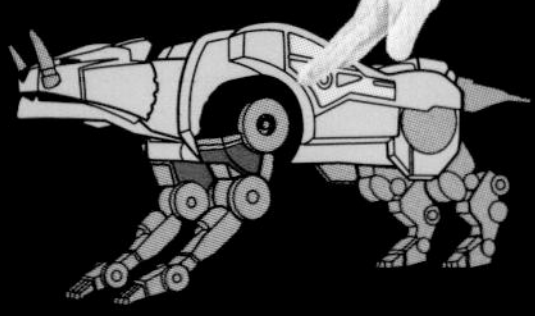

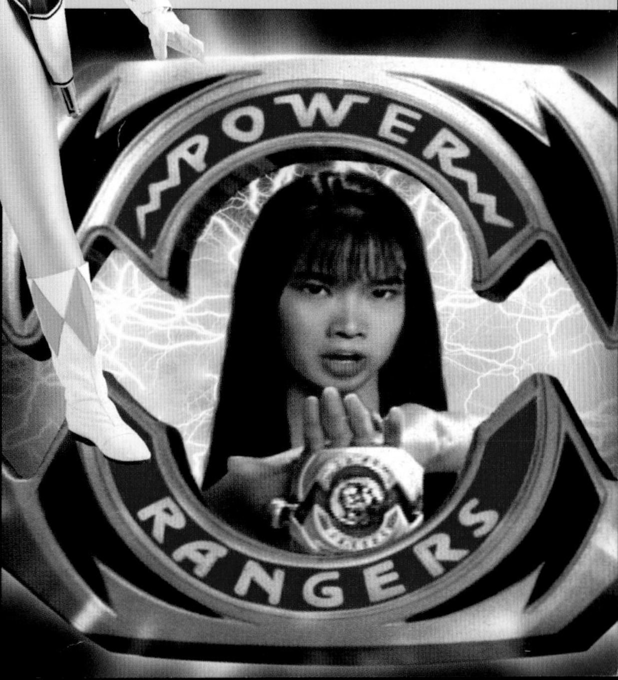
POWER
RANGERS

Weapon:
Power Daggers

Zord:
Sabertooth
Tiger
Dinozord

Notes:
Trini has a secret fear of heights.

SABAN'S MIGHTY MORPHIN POWER RANGERS

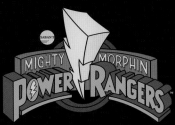

THE BLACK RANGER (ZACK TAYLOR)

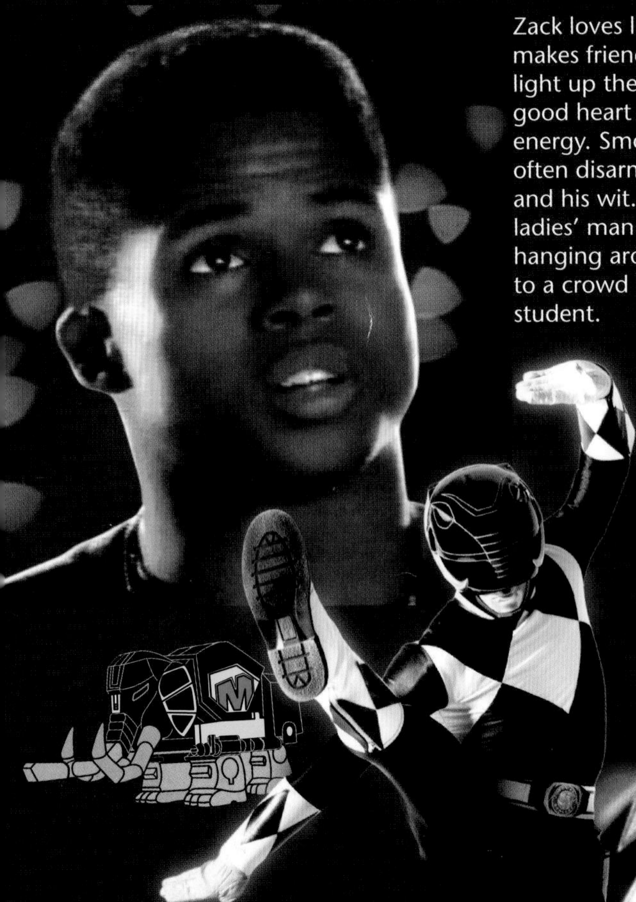

Zack loves life and always lives to the fullest. He makes friends with everyone and can always light up the room with his personality. He's got a good heart and a seemingly boundless supply of energy. Smooth talking and street-smart, he can often disarm his opponents with a quick smile and his wit. He also fancies himself quite the ladies' man. At school, Zack can often be found hanging around the music rooms, telling stories to a crowd in the quad, or helping out a fellow student.

Zack is intelligent and offers a good balance to Jason's often gung-ho style. Though he's very courageous, he will also often as the voice of caution in unclear situations. Intuition is Zack's guide and he'll often act based on hunches and instincts.

As a Power Ranger, Zack draws his power from the Mastadon and his weapon is the Power Axe.

Weapon:
Power Axe

Zord:
Mastodon
Dinozord

Notes:
Zack developed his own special fighting style: Hip Hop Kido.

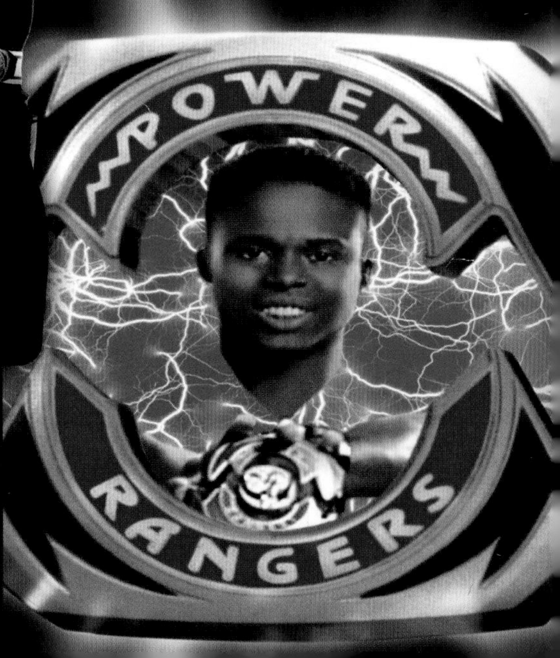
POWER
RANGERS

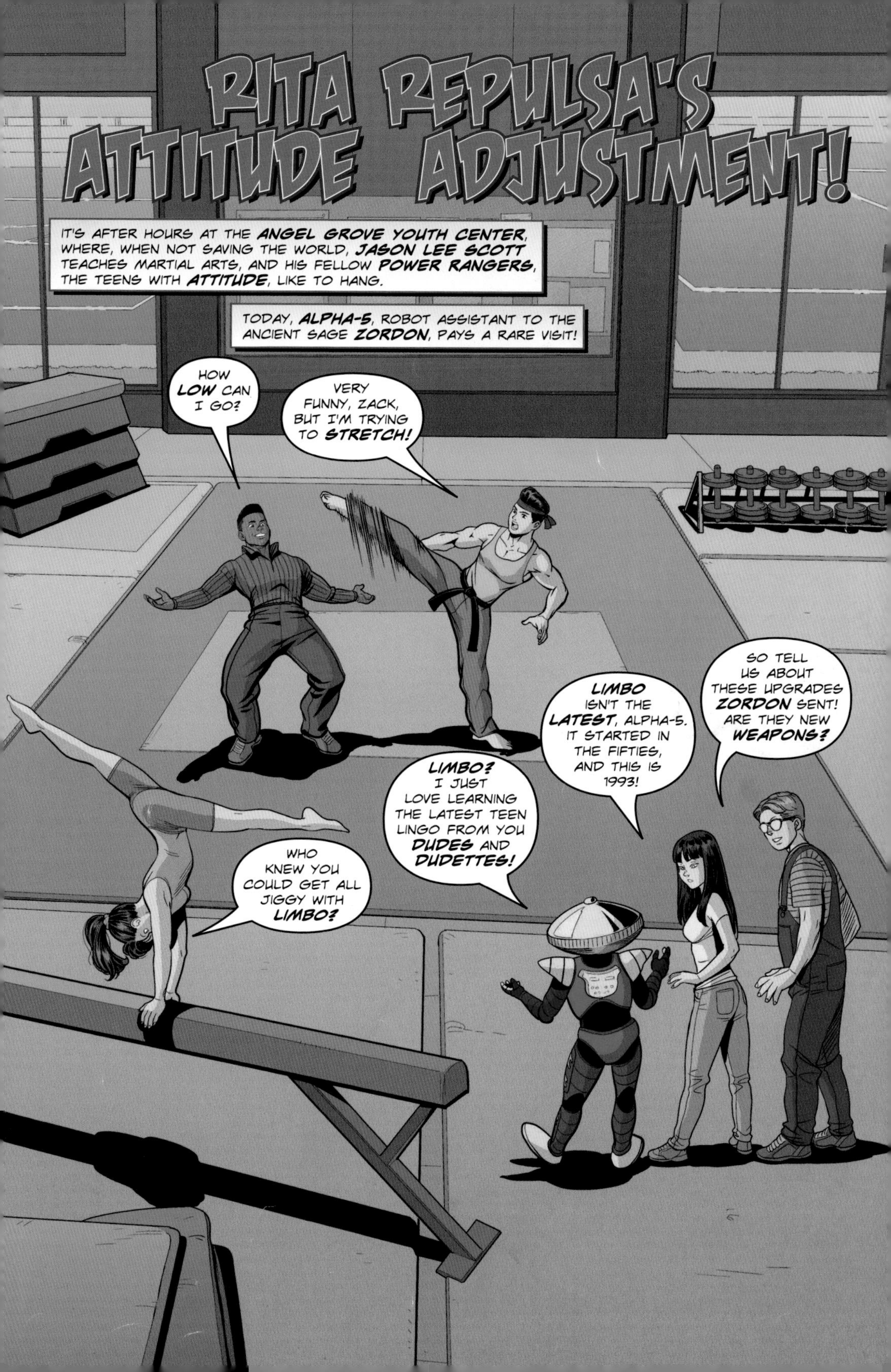
RITA REPULSA'S ATTITUDE ADJUSTMENT!
IT'S AFTER HOURS AT THE ANGEL GROVE YOUTH CENTER, WHERE, WHEN NOT SAVING THE WORLD, JASON LEE SCOTT TEACHES MARTIAL ARTS, AND HIS FELLOW POWER RANGERS, THE TEENS WITH ATTITUDE, LIKE TO HANG.
TODAY, ALPHA-5, ROBOT ASSISTANT TO THE ANCIENT SAGE ZORDON, PAYS A RARE VISIT!
HOW LOW CAN I GO?
VERY FUNNY, ZACK, BUT I'M TRYING TO STRETCH!
WHO KNEW YOU COULD GET ALL JIGGY WITH LIMBO?
LIMBO? I JUST LOVE LEARNING THE LATEST TEEN LINGO FROM YOU DUDES AND DUDETTES!
LIMBO ISN'T THE LATEST, ALPHA-5. IT STARTED IN THE FIFTIES, AND THIS IS 1993!
SO TELL US ABOUT THESE UPGRADES ZORDON SENT! ARE THEY NEW WEAPONS?

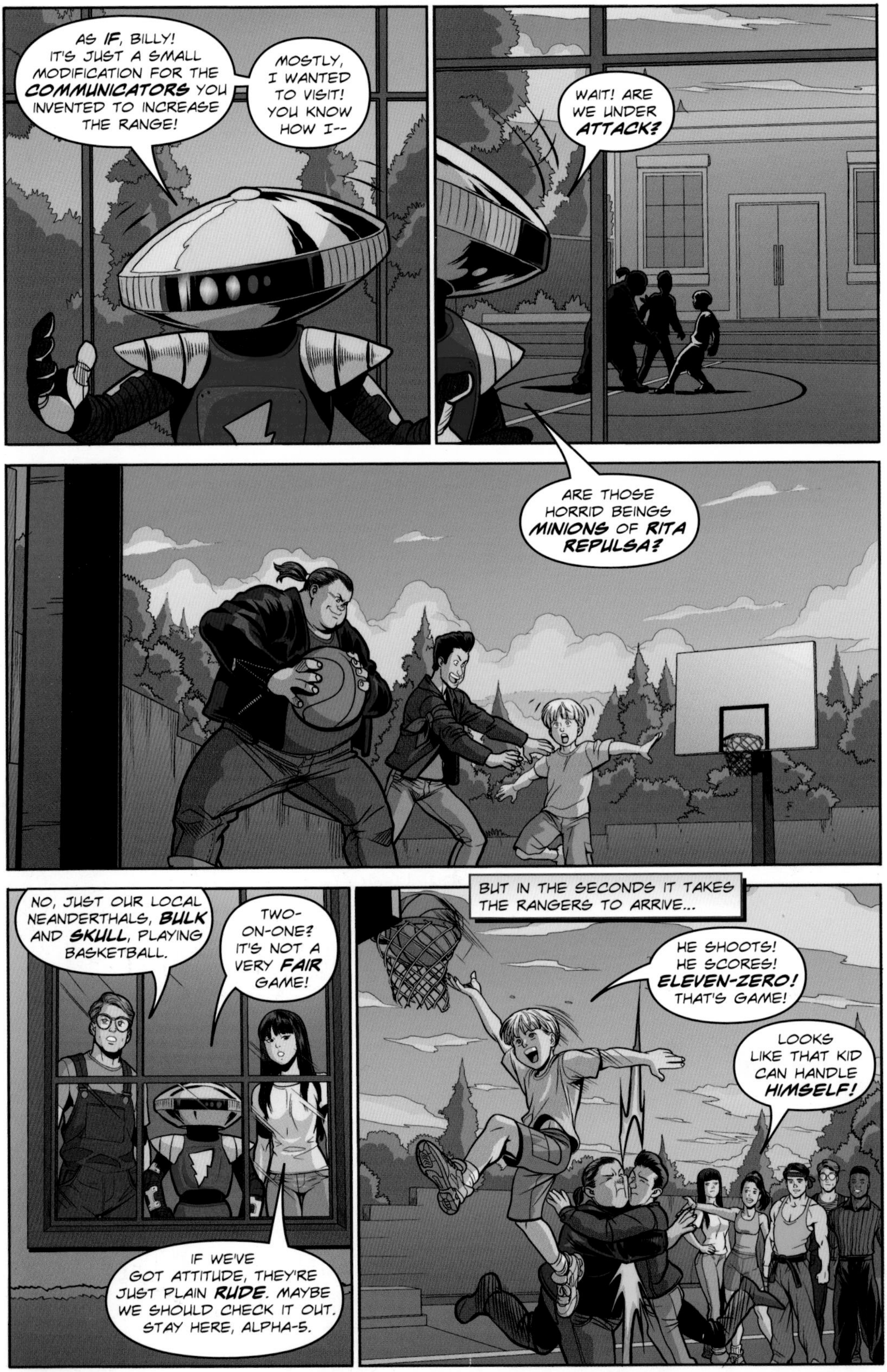
AS IF, BILLY! IT'S JUST A SMALL MODIFICATION FOR THE COMMUNICATORS YOU INVENTED TO INCREASE THE RANGE!
MOSTLY, I WANTED TO VISIT! YOU KNOW HOW I--
WAIT! ARE WE UNDER ATTACK?
ARE THOSE HORRID BEINGS MINIONS OF RITA REPULSA?
NO, JUST OUR LOCAL NEANDERTHALS, BULK AND SKULL, PLAYING BASKETBALL.
TWO-ON-ONE? IT'S NOT A VERY FAIR GAME!
IF WE'VE GOT ATTITUDE, THEY'RE JUST PLAIN RUDE. MAYBE WE SHOULD CHECK IT OUT. STAY HERE, ALPHA-5.
BUT IN THE SECONDS IT TAKES THE RANGERS TO ARRIVE...
HE SHOOTS! HE SCORES! ELEVEN-ZERO! THAT'S GAME!
LOOKS LIKE THAT KID CAN HANDLE HIMSELF!

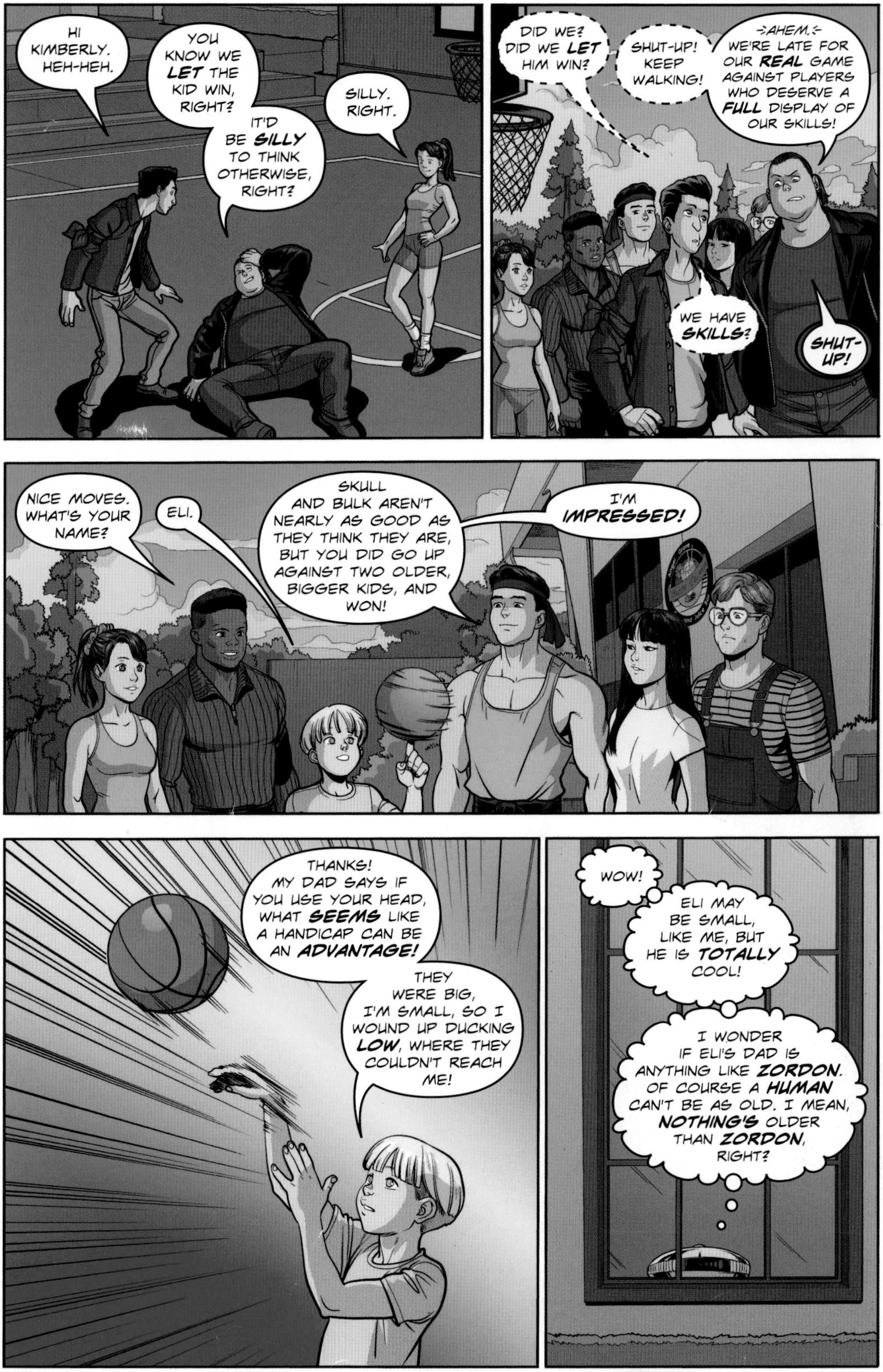
HI KIMBERLY. HEH-HEH.
YOU KNOW WE LET THE KID WIN, RIGHT?
IT'D BE SILLY TO THINK OTHERWISE, RIGHT?
SILLY. RIGHT.
DID WE? DID WE LET HIM WIN?
SHUT-UP! KEEP WALKING!
AHEM. WE'RE LATE FOR OUR REAL GAME AGAINST PLAYERS WHO DESERVE A FULL DISPLAY OF OUR SKILLS!
WE HAVE SKILLS?
SHUT-UP!
NICE MOVES. WHAT'S YOUR NAME?
ELI.
SKULL AND BULK AREN'T NEARLY AS GOOD AS THEY THINK THEY ARE, BUT YOU DID GO UP AGAINST TWO OLDER, BIGGER KIDS, AND WON!
I'M IMPRESSED!
THANKS! MY DAD SAYS IF YOU USE YOUR HEAD, WHAT SEEMS LIKE A HANDICAP CAN BE AN ADVANTAGE!
THEY WERE BIG, I'M SMALL, SO I WOUND UP DUCKING LOW, WHERE THEY COULDN'T REACH ME!
WOW!
ELI MAY BE SMALL, LIKE ME, BUT HE IS TOTALLY COOL!
I WONDER IF ELI'S DAD IS ANYTHING LIKE ZORDON. OF COURSE A HUMAN CAN'T BE AS OLD. I MEAN, NOTHING'S OLDER THAN ZORDON, RIGHT?

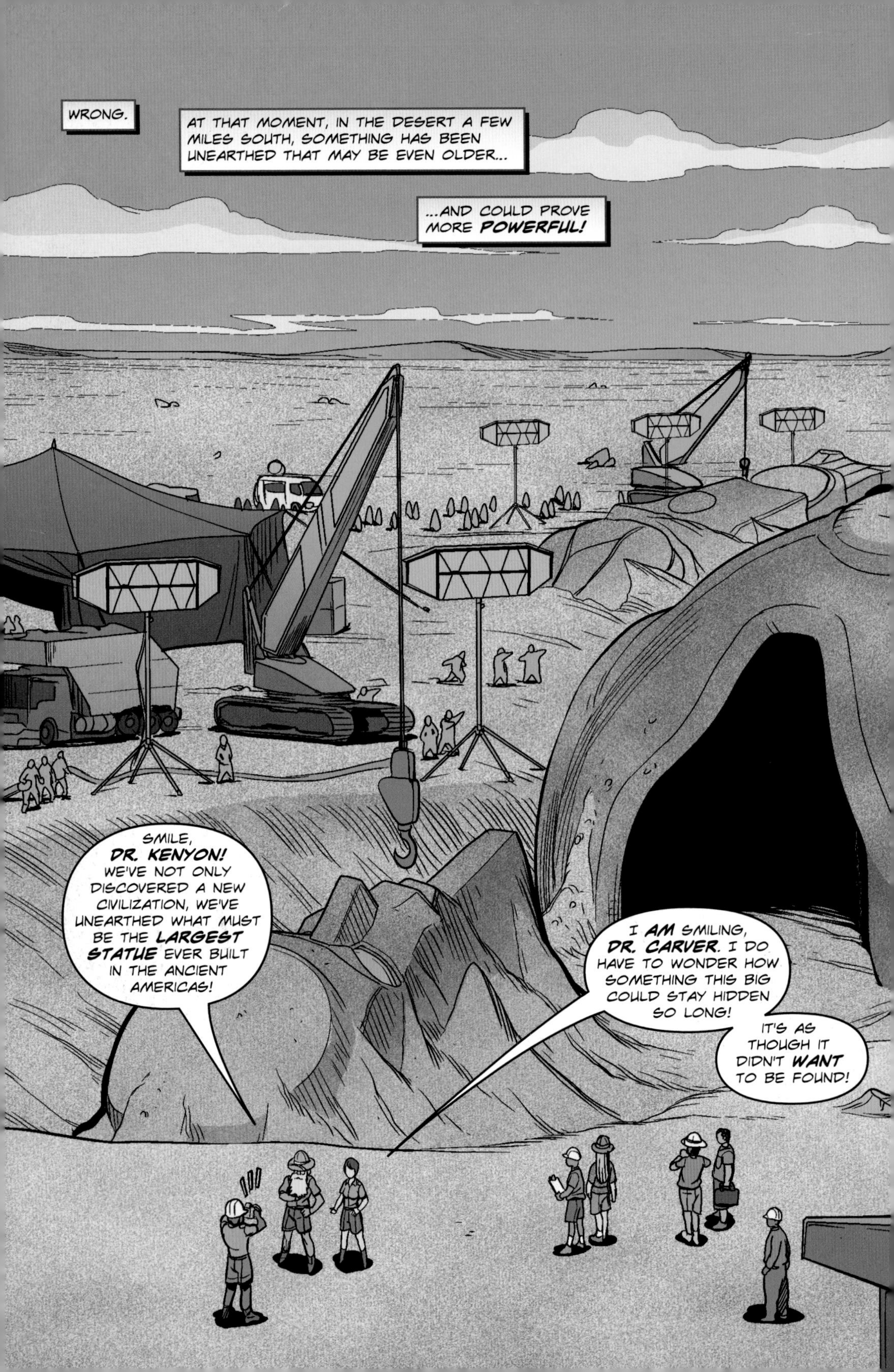
WRONG.
AT THAT MOMENT, IN THE DESERT A FEW MILES SOUTH, SOMETHING HAS BEEN UNEARTHED THAT MAY BE EVEN OLDER...
...AND COULD PROVE MORE **POWERFUL!**
SMILE, **DR. KENYON!** WE'VE NOT ONLY DISCOVERED A NEW CIVILIZATION, WE'VE UNEARTHED WHAT MUST BE THE **LARGEST STATUE** EVER BUILT IN THE ANCIENT AMERICAS!
I **AM** SMILING, **DR. CARVER**. I DO HAVE TO WONDER HOW SOMETHING THIS BIG COULD STAY HIDDEN SO LONG!
IT'S AS THOUGH IT DIDN'T **WANT** TO BE FOUND!

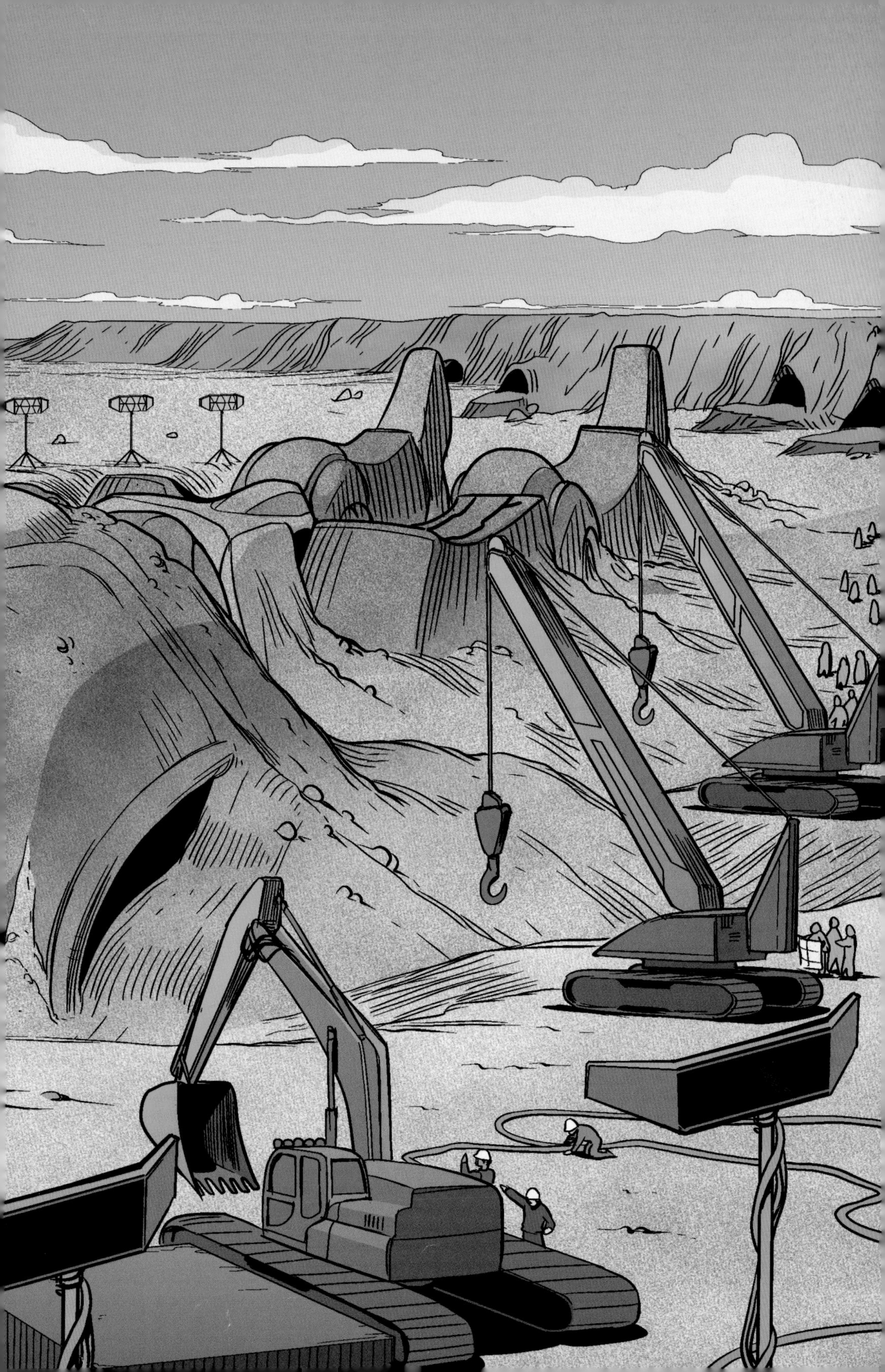

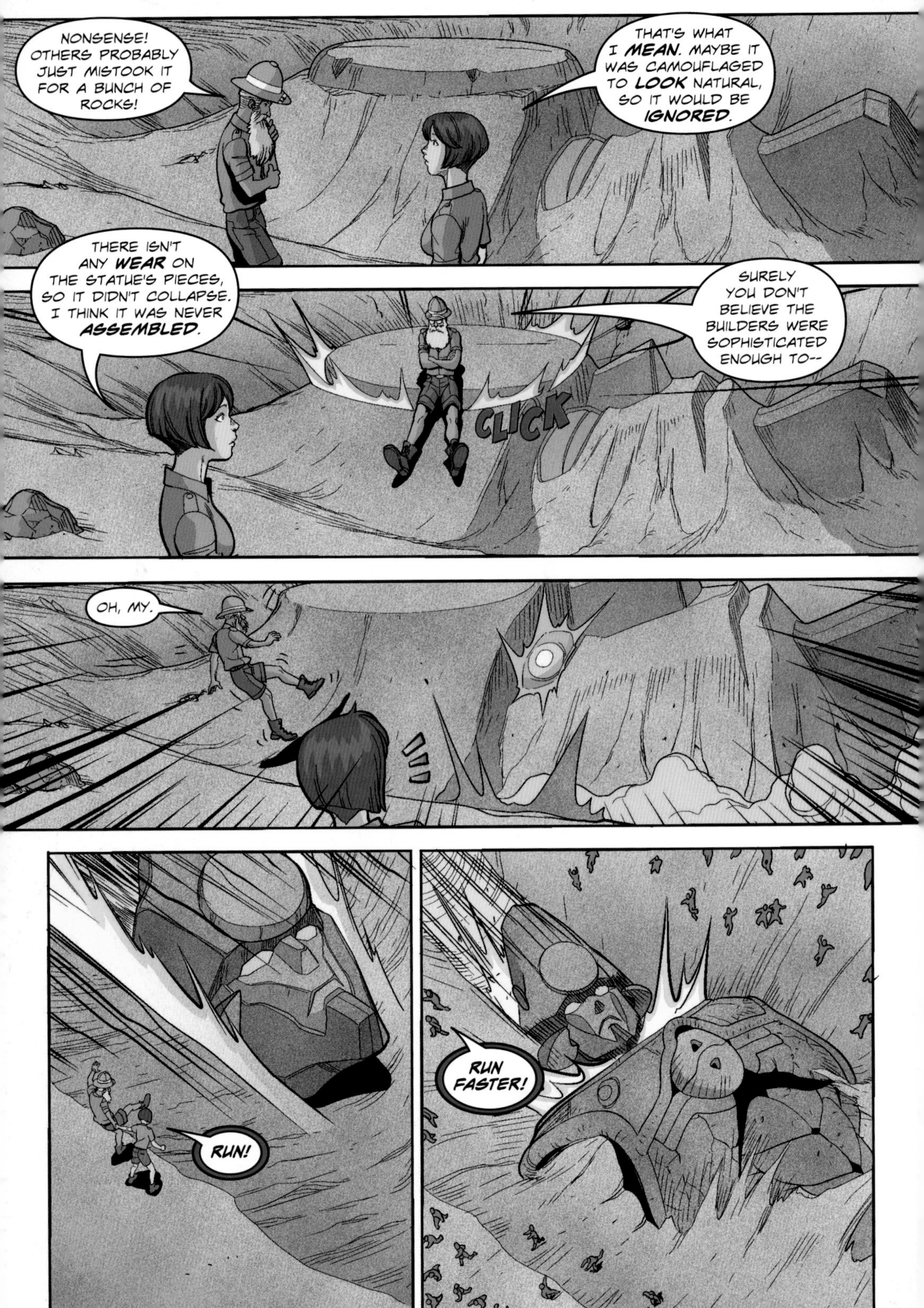
NONSENSE! OTHERS PROBABLY JUST MISTOOK IT FOR A BUNCH OF ROCKS!
THAT'S WHAT I MEAN. MAYBE IT WAS CAMOUFLAGED TO LOOK NATURAL, SO IT WOULD BE IGNORED.
THERE ISN'T ANY WEAR ON THE STATUE'S PIECES, SO IT DIDN'T COLLAPSE. I THINK IT WAS NEVER ASSEMBLED.
SURELY YOU DON'T BELIEVE THE BUILDERS WERE SOPHISTICATED ENOUGH TO--
CLICK
OH, MY.
RUN!
RUN FASTER!

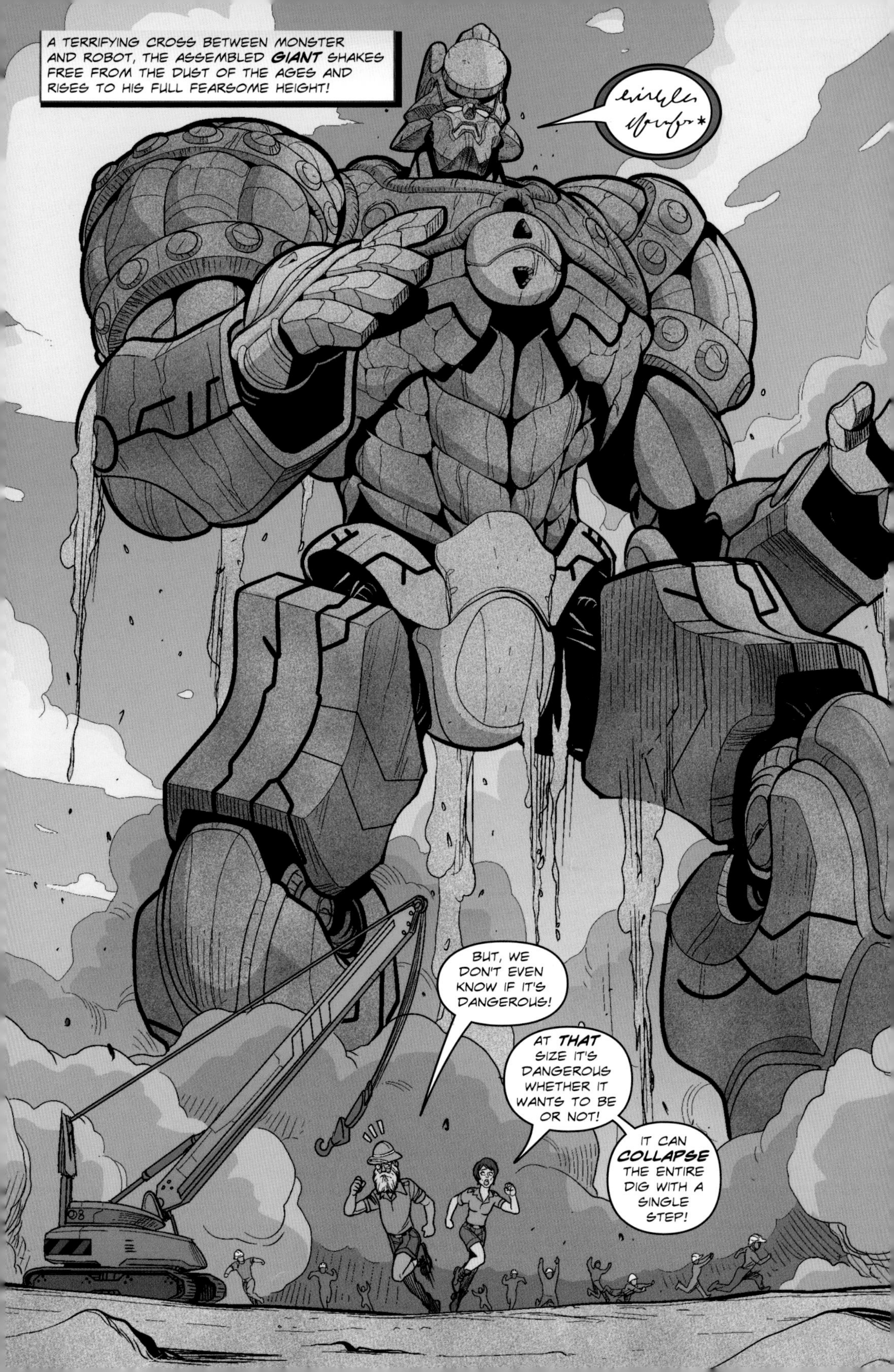
A TERRIFYING CROSS BETWEEN MONSTER AND ROBOT, THE ASSEMBLED GIANT SHAKES FREE FROM THE DUST OF THE AGES AND RISES TO HIS FULL FEARSOME HEIGHT!
BUT, WE DON'T EVEN KNOW IF IT'S DANGEROUS!
AT THAT SIZE IT'S DANGEROUS WHETHER IT WANTS TO BE OR NOT!
IT CAN COLLAPSE THE ENTIRE DIG WITH A SINGLE STEP!
!!!

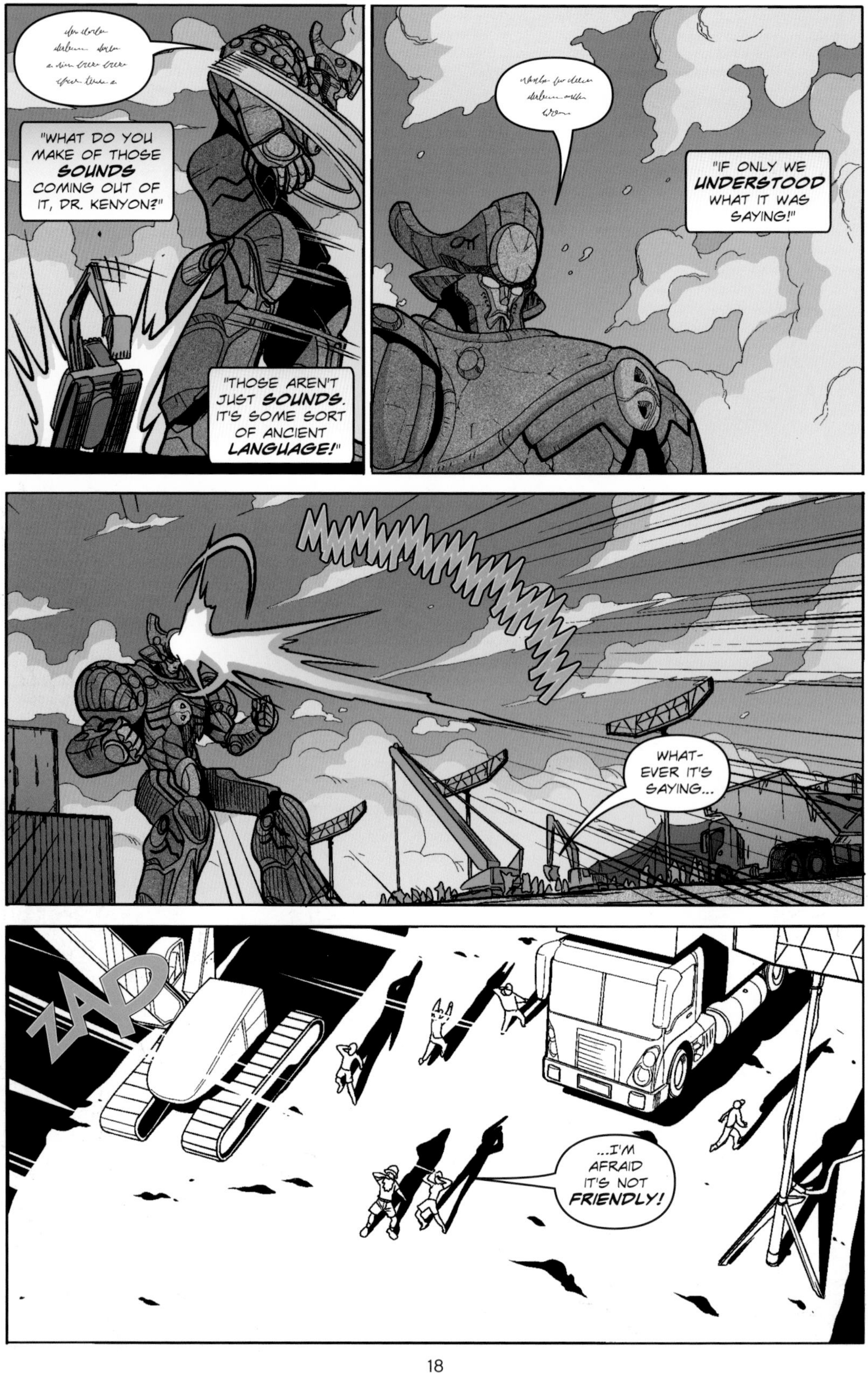
"WHAT DO YOU MAKE OF THOSE SOUNDS COMING OUT OF IT, DR. KENYON?"
"THOSE AREN'T JUST SOUNDS. IT'S SOME SORT OF ANCIENT LANGUAGE!"
"IF ONLY WE UNDERSTOOD WHAT IT WAS SAYING!"
MMMMMMMMMMMMMM
WHAT-EVER IT'S SAYING...
ZAP
...I'M AFRAID IT'S NOT FRIENDLY!

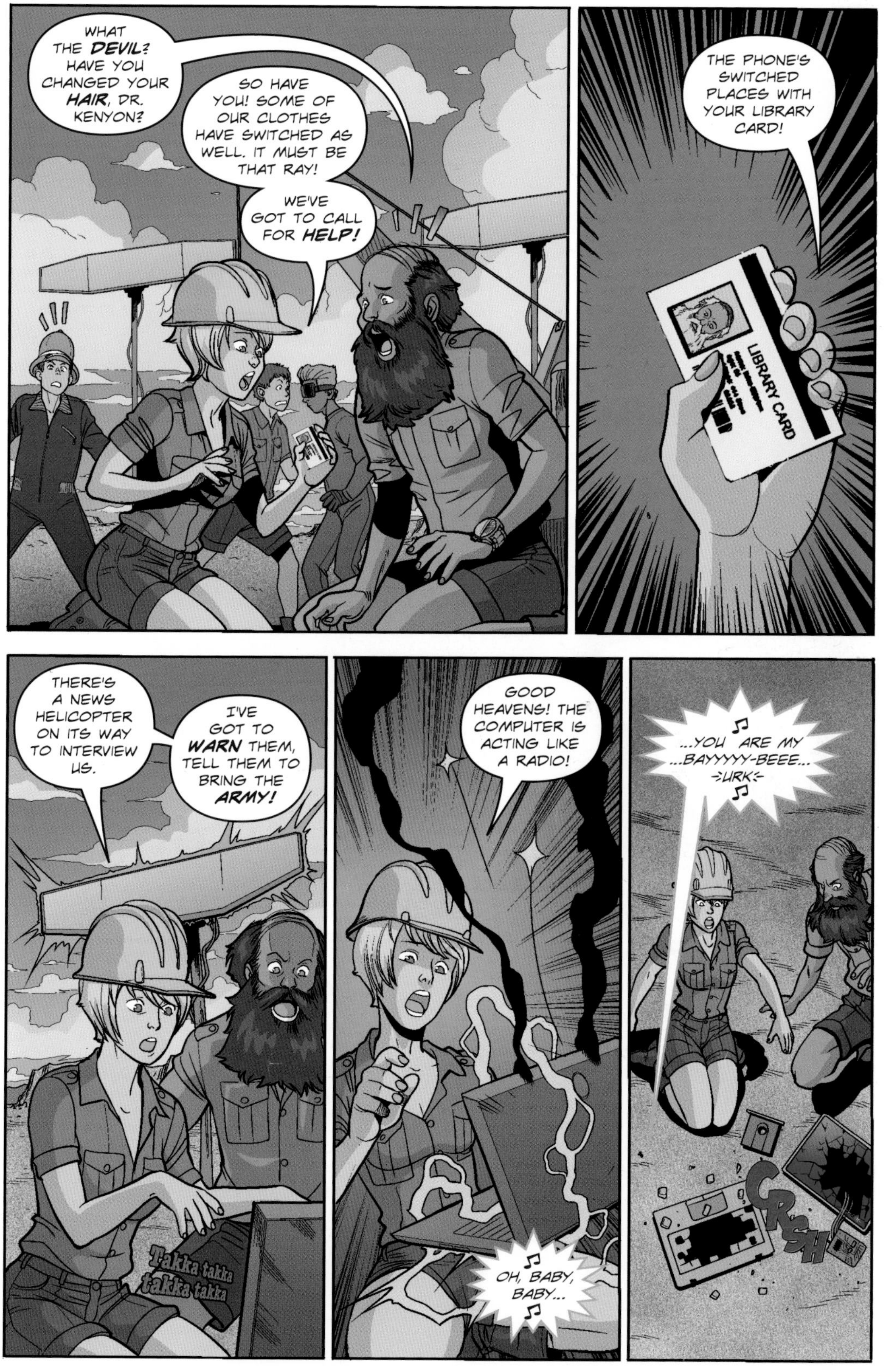
WHAT THE **DEVIL**? HAVE YOU CHANGED YOUR **HAIR**, DR. KENYON?
SO HAVE YOU! SOME OF OUR CLOTHES HAVE SWITCHED AS WELL. IT MUST BE THAT RAY!
WE'VE GOT TO CALL FOR **HELP!**
THE PHONE'S SWITCHED PLACES WITH YOUR LIBRARY CARD!
LIBRARY CARD
THERE'S A NEWS HELICOPTER ON ITS WAY TO INTERVIEW US.
I'VE GOT TO **WARN** THEM, TELL THEM TO BRING THE **ARMY!**
Takka takka takka takka
GOOD HEAVENS! THE COMPUTER IS ACTING LIKE A RADIO!
♫ OH, BABY, BABY... ♫
♫ ...YOU ARE MY ...BAYYYYY-BEEE... -URK- ♫
CRSH

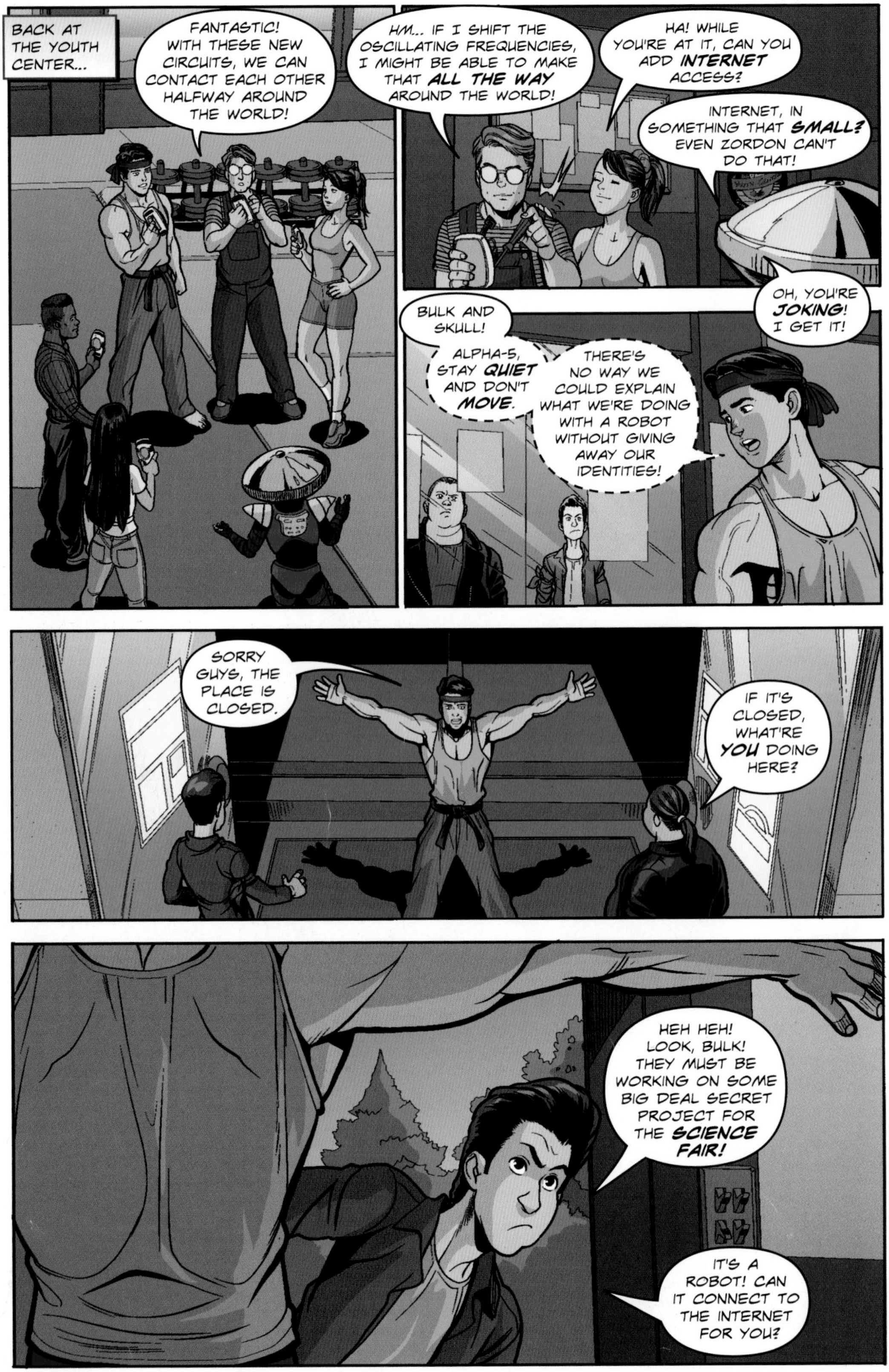
BACK AT THE YOUTH CENTER...
FANTASTIC! WITH THESE NEW CIRCUITS, WE CAN CONTACT EACH OTHER HALFWAY AROUND THE WORLD!
HM... IF I SHIFT THE OSCILLATING FREQUENCIES, I MIGHT BE ABLE TO MAKE THAT ALL THE WAY AROUND THE WORLD!
HA! WHILE YOU'RE AT IT, CAN YOU ADD INTERNET ACCESS?
INTERNET, IN SOMETHING THAT SMALL? EVEN ZORDON CAN'T DO THAT!
OH, YOU'RE JOKING! I GET IT!
BULK AND SKULL!
ALPHA-5, STAY QUIET AND DON'T MOVE.
THERE'S NO WAY WE COULD EXPLAIN WHAT WE'RE DOING WITH A ROBOT WITHOUT GIVING AWAY OUR IDENTITIES!
SORRY GUYS, THE PLACE IS CLOSED.
IF IT'S CLOSED, WHAT'RE YOU DOING HERE?
HEH HEH! LOOK, BULK! THEY MUST BE WORKING ON SOME BIG DEAL SECRET PROJECT FOR THE SCIENCE FAIR!
IT'S A ROBOT! CAN IT CONNECT TO THE INTERNET FOR YOU?

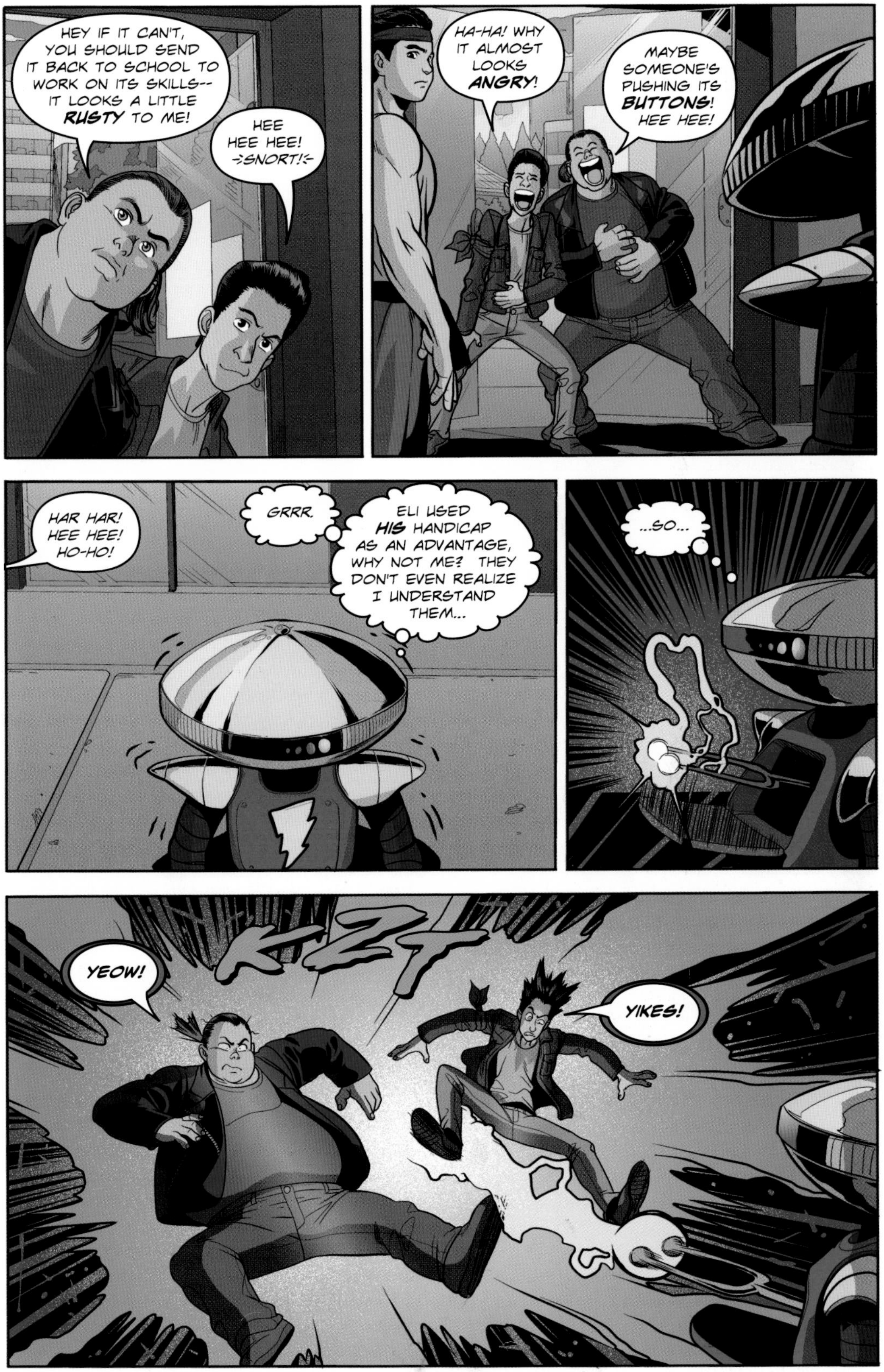

HEY IF IT CAN'T, YOU SHOULD SEND IT BACK TO SCHOOL TO WORK ON ITS SKILLS-- IT LOOKS A LITTLE RUSTY TO ME!
HEE HEE HEE! -SNORT!-
HA-HA! WHY IT ALMOST LOOKS ANGRY!
MAYBE SOMEONE'S PUSHING ITS BUTTONS! HEE HEE!
HAR HAR! HEE HEE! HO-HO!
GRRR.
ELI USED HIS HANDICAP AS AN ADVANTAGE, WHY NOT ME? THEY DON'T EVEN REALIZE I UNDERSTAND THEM...
...SO...
KZZT
YEOW!
YIKES!

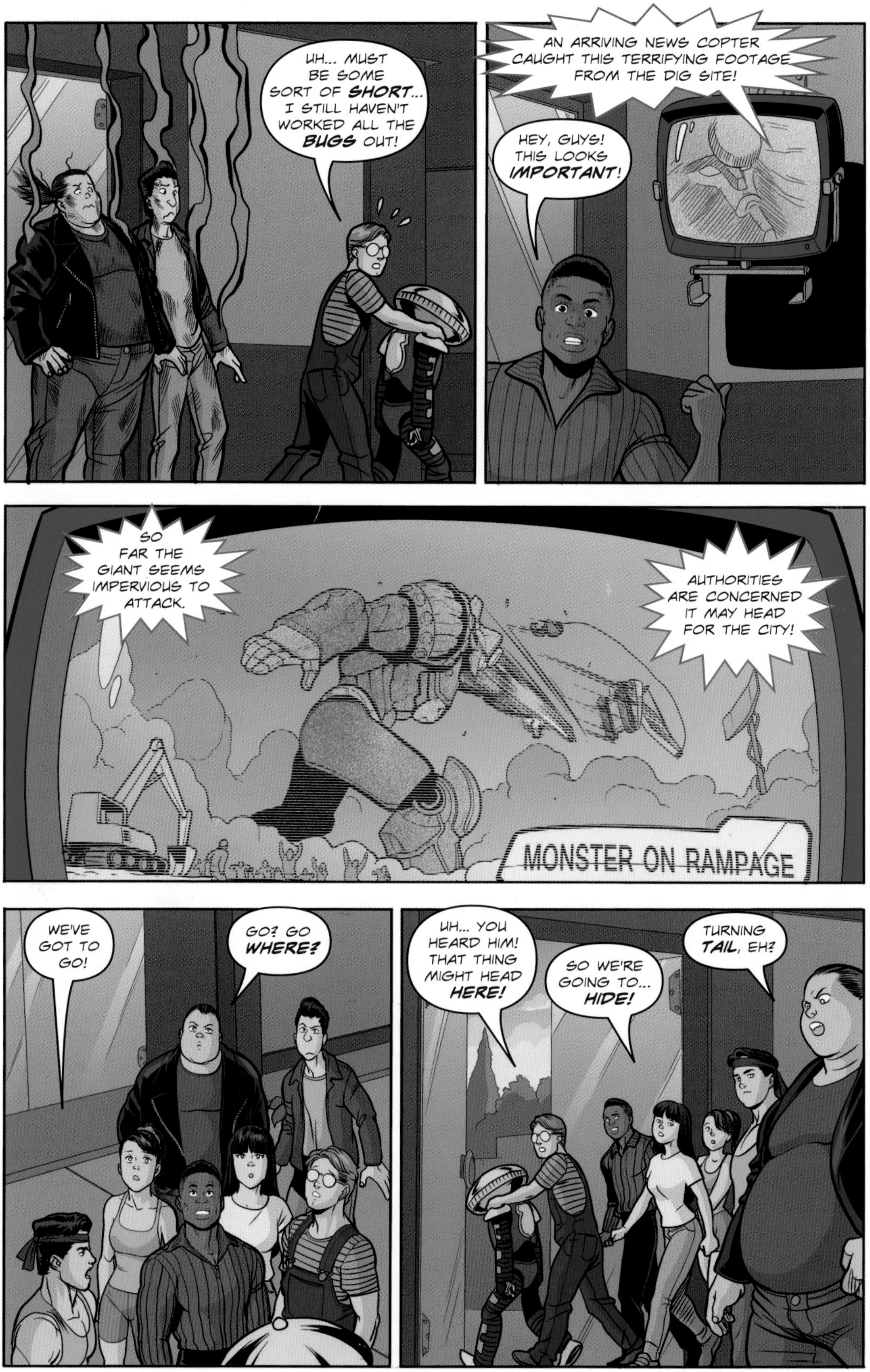

UH... MUST BE SOME SORT OF SHORT... I STILL HAVEN'T WORKED ALL THE BUGS OUT!
AN ARRIVING NEWS COPTER CAUGHT THIS TERRIFYING FOOTAGE FROM THE DIG SITE!
HEY, GUYS! THIS LOOKS IMPORTANT!
SO FAR THE GIANT SEEMS IMPERVIOUS TO ATTACK.
AUTHORITIES ARE CONCERNED IT MAY HEAD FOR THE CITY!
MONSTER ON RAMPAGE
WE'VE GOT TO GO!
GO? GO WHERE?
UH... YOU HEARD HIM! THAT THING MIGHT HEAD HERE!
SO WE'RE GOING TO... HIDE!
TURNING TAIL, EH?

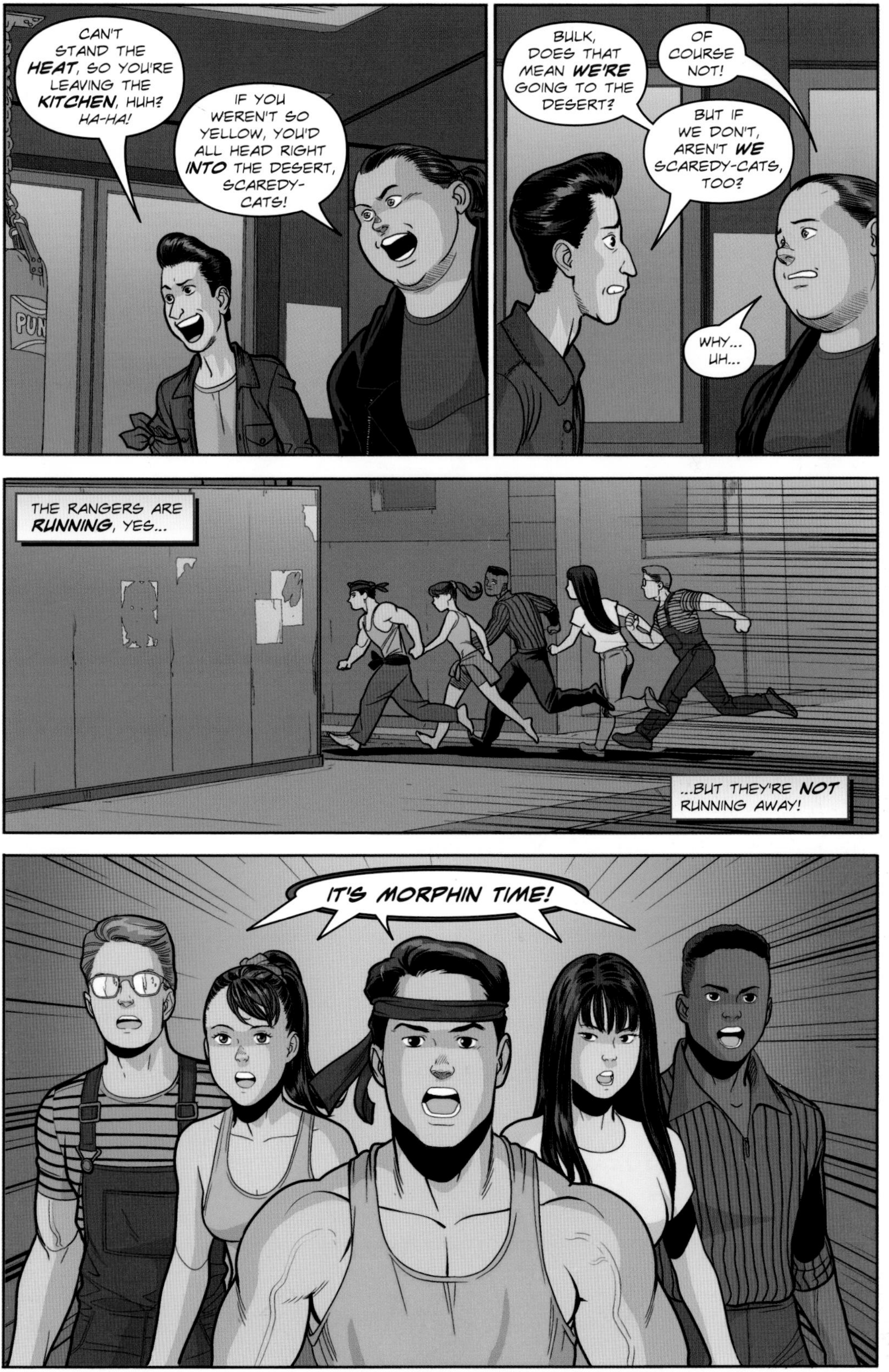
CAN'T STAND THE **HEAT**, SO YOU'RE LEAVING THE **KITCHEN**, HUH? HA-HA!
IF YOU WEREN'T SO YELLOW, YOU'D ALL HEAD RIGHT **INTO** THE DESERT, SCAREDY-CATS!
BULK, DOES THAT MEAN **WE'RE** GOING TO THE DESERT?
OF COURSE NOT!
BUT IF WE DON'T, AREN'T **WE** SCAREDY-CATS, TOO?
WHY... UH...
THE RANGERS ARE **RUNNING**, YES...
...BUT THEY'RE **NOT** RUNNING AWAY!
IT'S MORPHIN TIME!

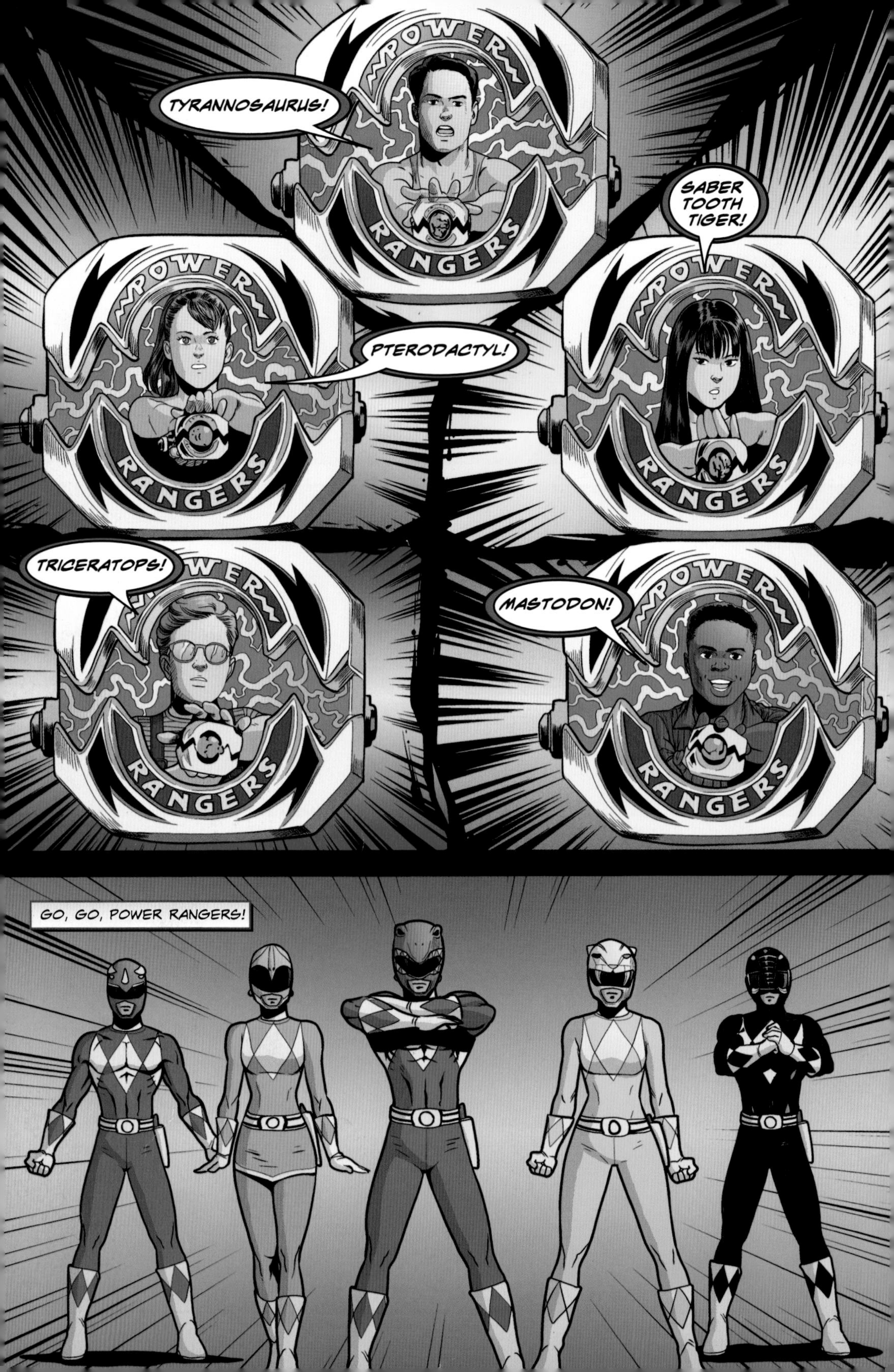
TYRANNOSAURUS!
SABER TOOTH TIGER!
PTERODACTYL!
TRICERATOPS!
MASTODON!
GO, GO, POWER RANGERS!

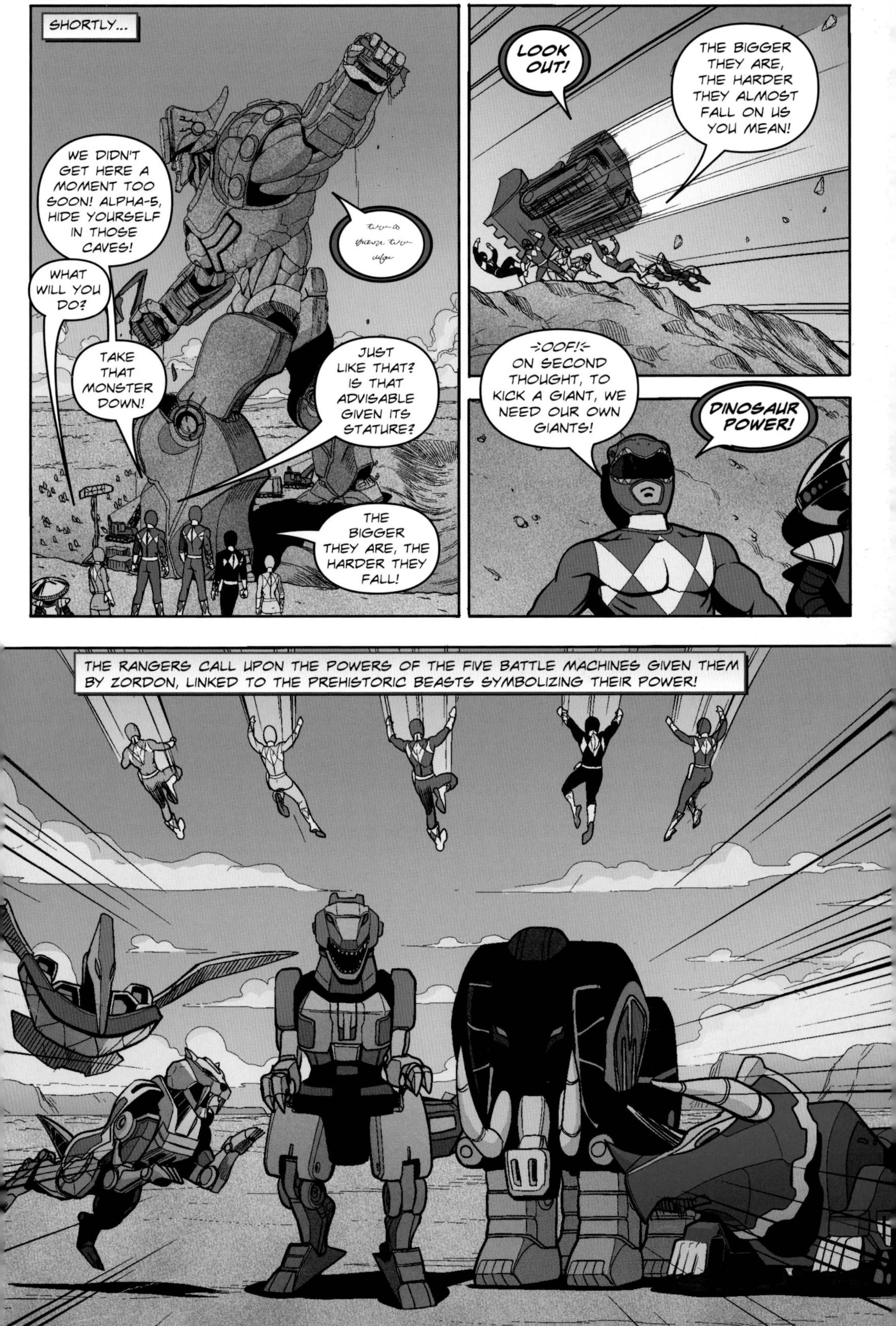
SHORTLY...
WE DIDN'T GET HERE A MOMENT TOO SOON! ALPHA-5, HIDE YOURSELF IN THOSE CAVES!
WHAT WILL YOU DO?
TAKE THAT MONSTER DOWN!
JUST LIKE THAT? IS THAT ADVISABLE GIVEN ITS STATURE?
THE BIGGER THEY ARE, THE HARDER THEY FALL!
LOOK OUT!
THE BIGGER THEY ARE, THE HARDER THEY ALMOST FALL ON US YOU MEAN!
OOF! ON SECOND THOUGHT, TO KICK A GIANT, WE NEED OUR OWN GIANTS!
DINOSAUR POWER!
THE RANGERS CALL UPON THE POWERS OF THE FIVE BATTLE MACHINES GIVEN THEM BY ZORDON, LINKED TO THE PREHISTORIC BEASTS SYMBOLIZING THEIR POWER!

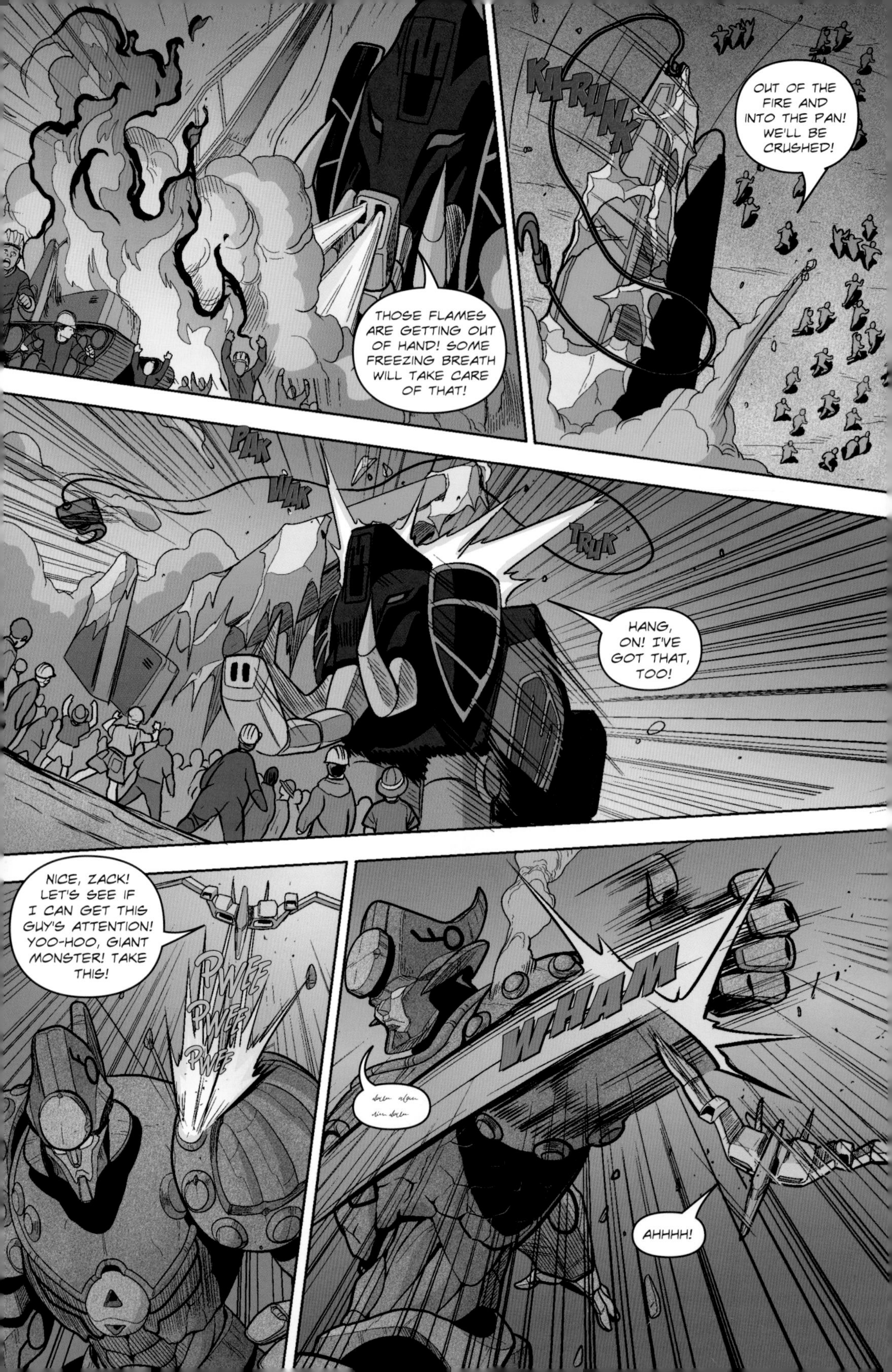
THOSE FLAMES ARE GETTING OUT OF HAND! SOME FREEZING BREATH WILL TAKE CARE OF THAT!
KA-RUNK
OUT OF THE FIRE AND INTO THE PAN! WE'LL BE CRUSHED!
PAK
WAK
TRUK
HANG, ON! I'VE GOT THAT, TOO!
NICE, ZACK! LET'S SEE IF I CAN GET THIS GUY'S ATTENTION! YOO-HOO, GIANT MONSTER! TAKE THIS!
PWEE
PWEE
PWEE
WHAM
AHHHH!

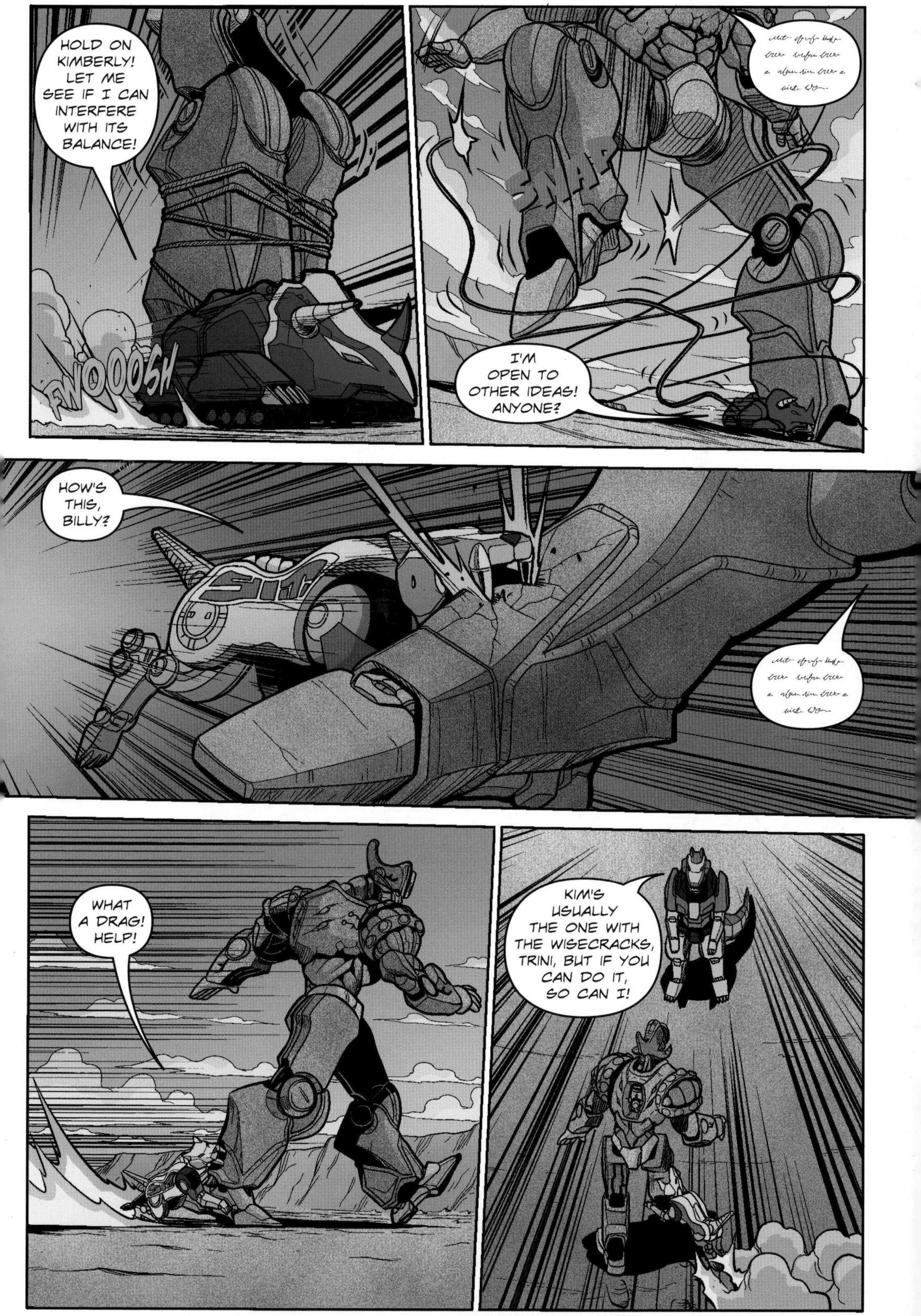
HOLD ON KIMBERLY! LET ME SEE IF I CAN INTERFERE WITH ITS BALANCE!
FWOOOSH
SNAP
I'M OPEN TO OTHER IDEAS! ANYONE?
HOW'S THIS, BILLY?
WHAT A DRAG! HELP!
KIM'S USUALLY THE ONE WITH THE WISECRACKS, TRINI, BUT IF YOU CAN DO IT, SO CAN I!

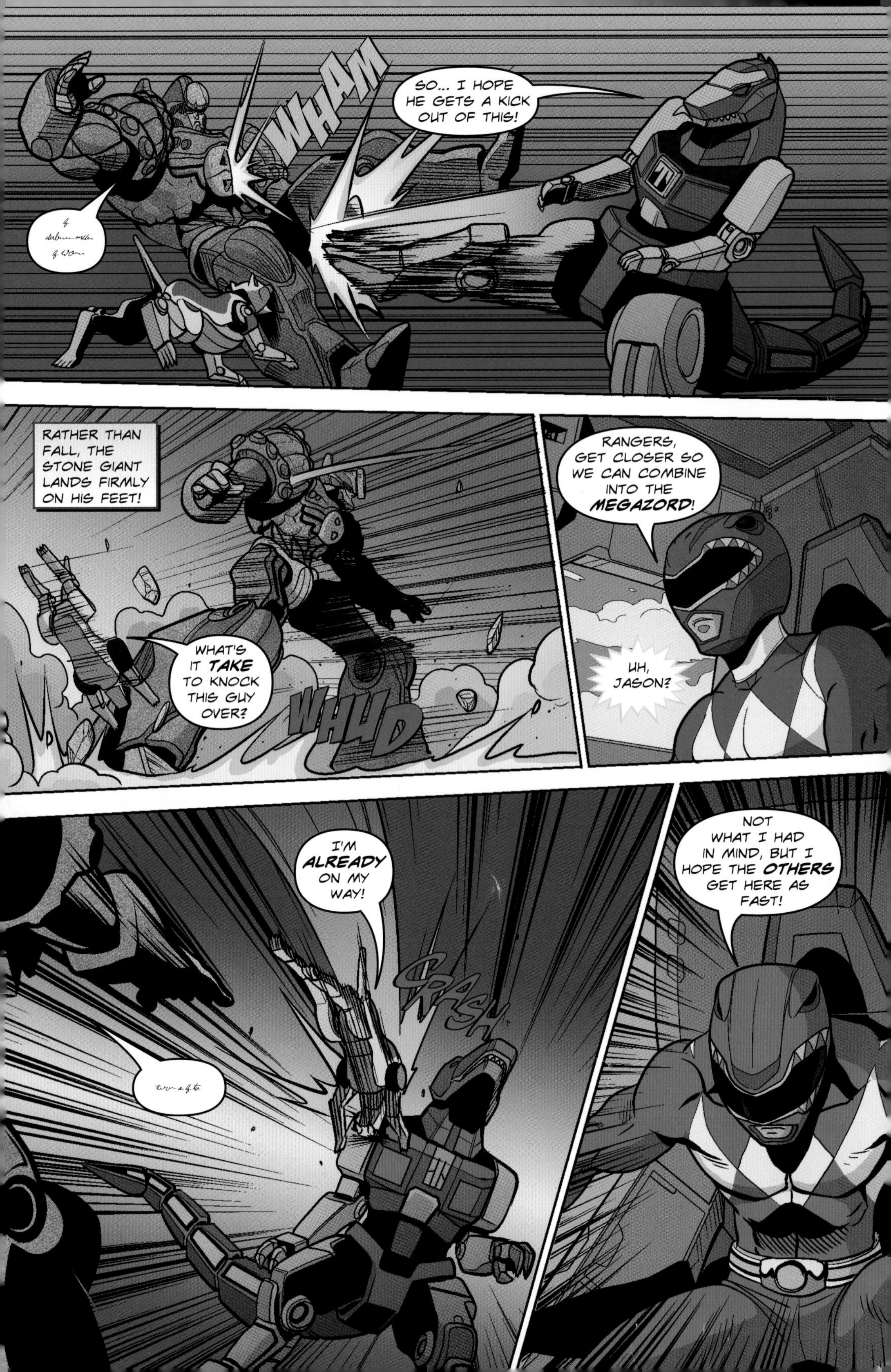
WHAM
SO... I HOPE HE GETS A KICK OUT OF THIS!
RATHER THAN FALL, THE STONE GIANT LANDS FIRMLY ON HIS FEET!
WHAT'S IT TAKE TO KNOCK THIS GUY OVER?
WHUD
RANGERS, GET CLOSER SO WE CAN COMBINE INTO THE MEGAZORD!
UH, JASON?
I'M ALREADY ON MY WAY!
CRASH
NOT WHAT I HAD IN MIND, BUT I HOPE THE OTHERS GET HERE AS FAST!

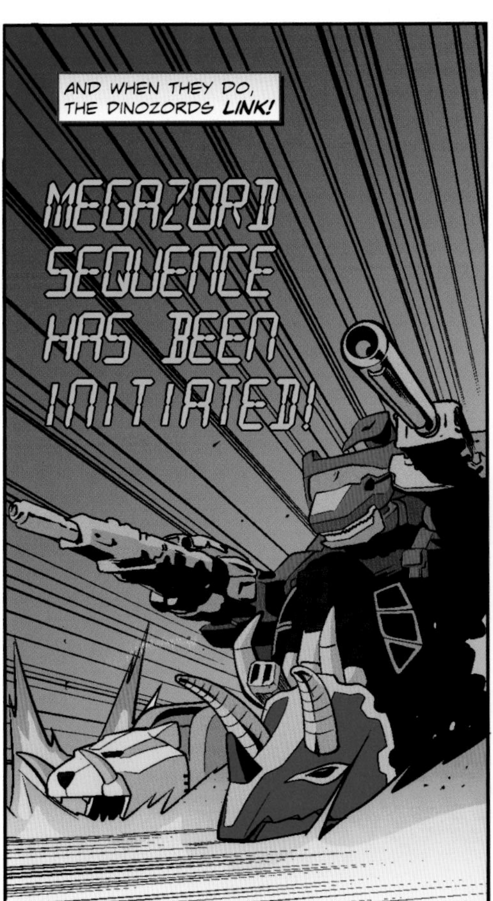
AND WHEN THEY DO, THE DINOZORDS LINK!
MEGAZORD SEQUENCE HAS BEEN INITIATED!

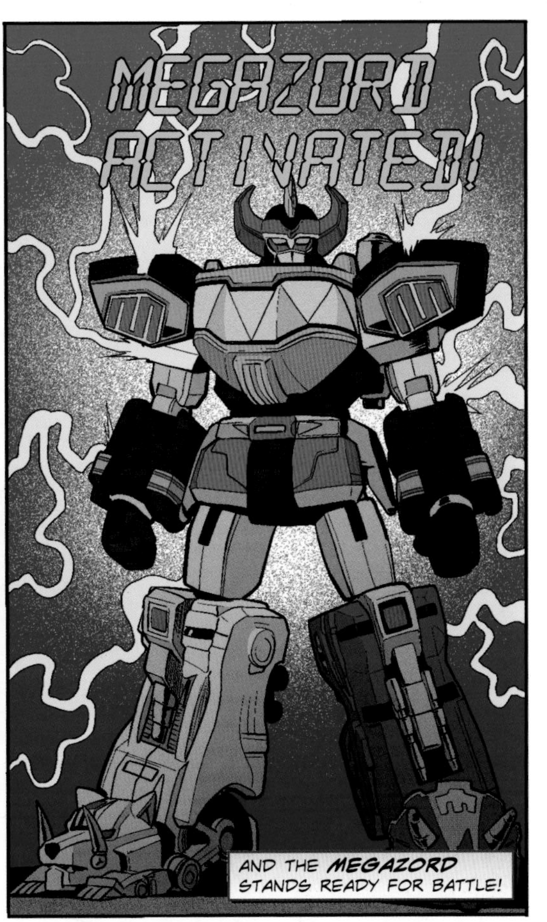
MEGAZORD ACTIVATED!
AND THE MEGAZORD STANDS READY FOR BATTLE!

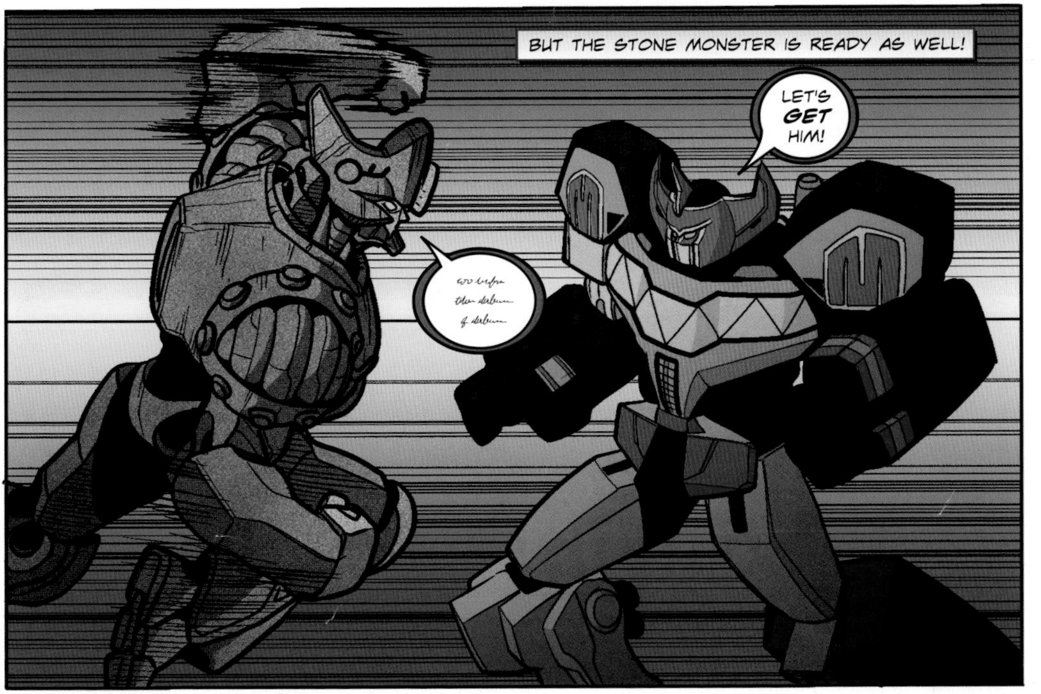
BUT THE STONE MONSTER IS READY AS WELL!
LET'S GET HIM!

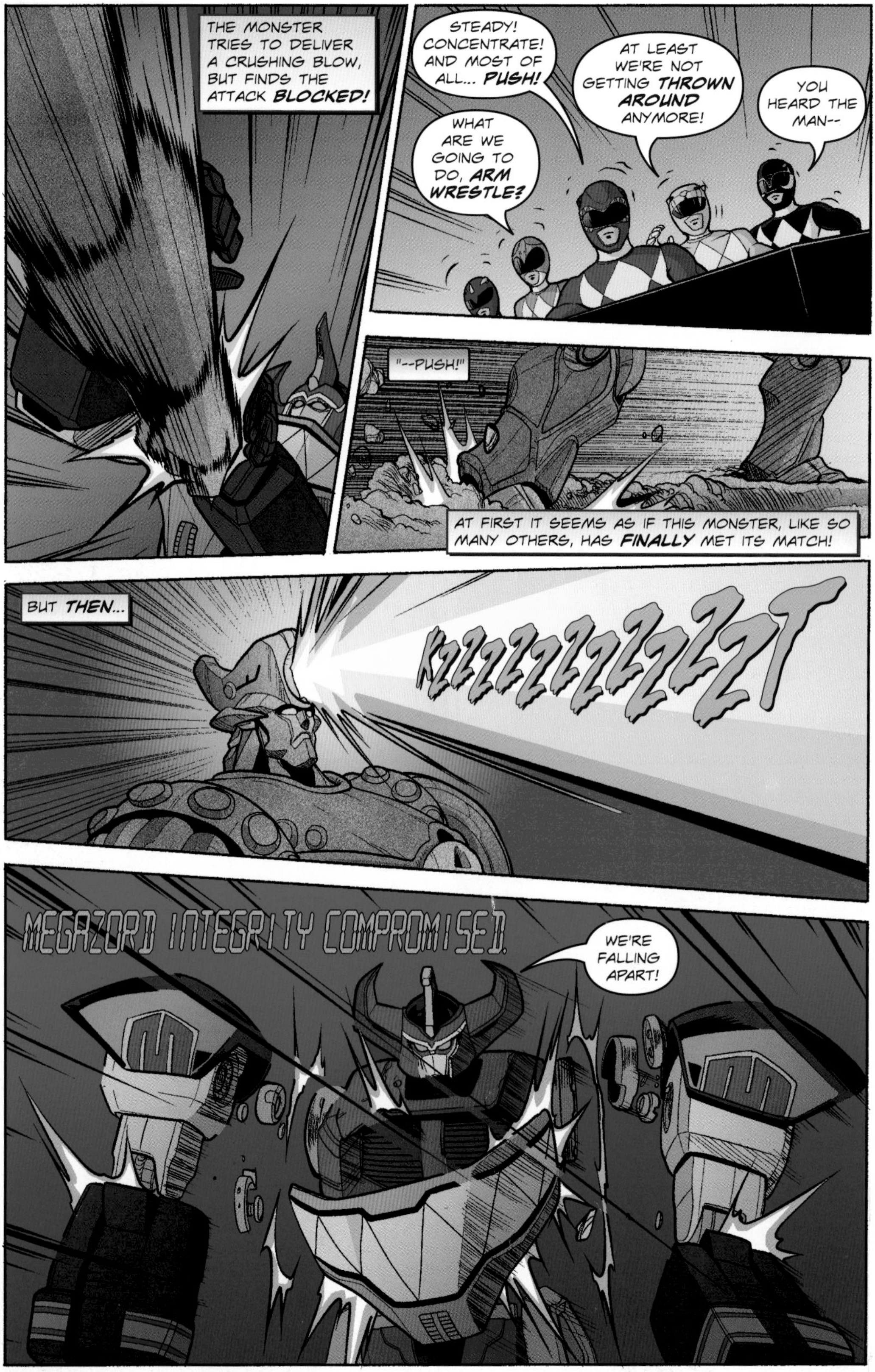
THE MONSTER TRIES TO DELIVER A CRUSHING BLOW, BUT FINDS THE ATTACK BLOCKED!
STEADY! CONCENTRATE! AND MOST OF ALL... PUSH!
WHAT ARE WE GOING TO DO, ARM WRESTLE?
AT LEAST WE'RE NOT GETTING THROWN AROUND ANYMORE!
YOU HEARD THE MAN--
"--PUSH!"
AT FIRST IT SEEMS AS IF THIS MONSTER, LIKE SO MANY OTHERS, HAS FINALLY MET ITS MATCH!
BUT THEN...
KZZZZZZZZZZZT
MEGAZORD INTEGRITY COMPROMISED.
WE'RE FALLING APART!

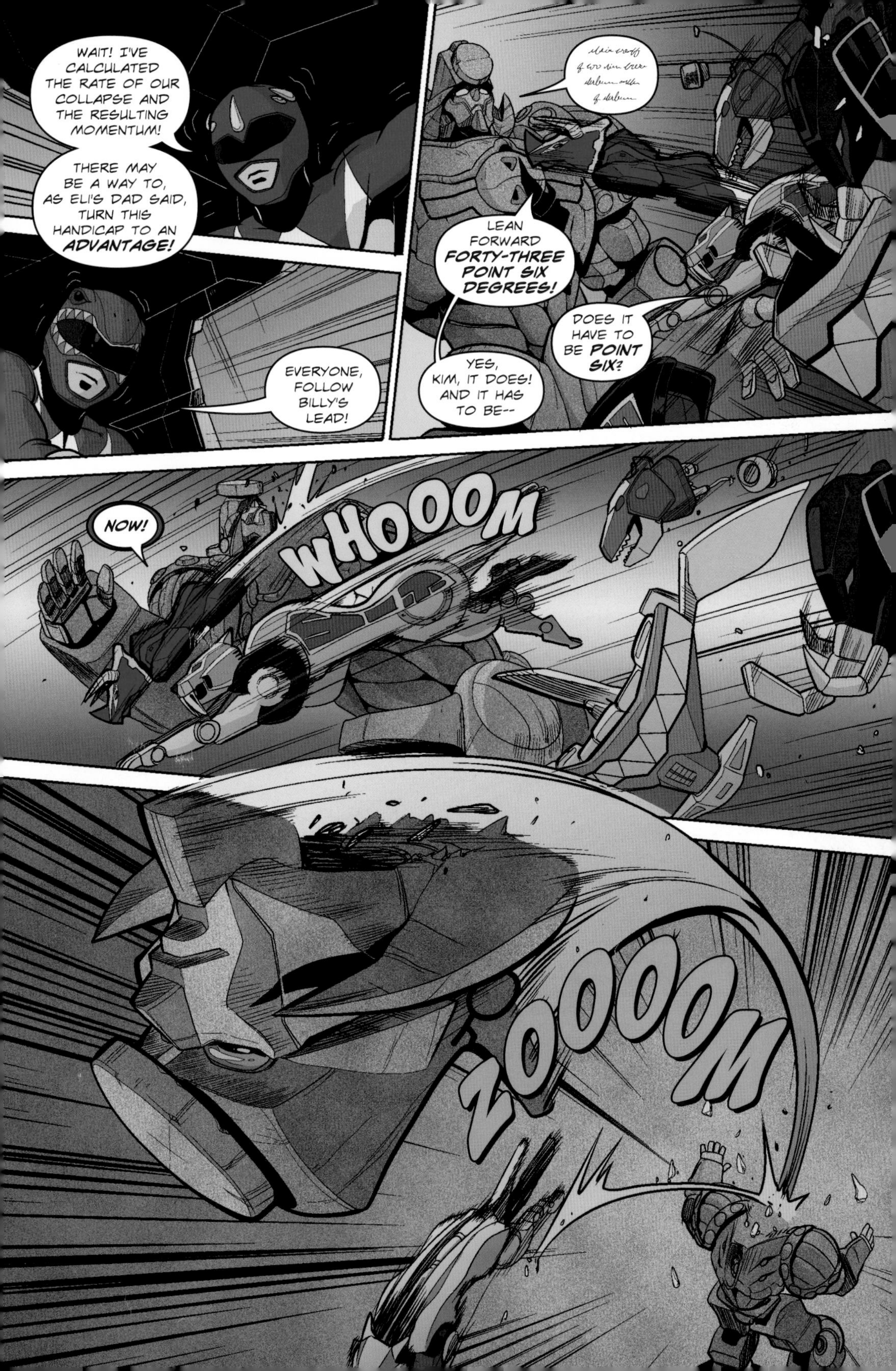
WAIT! I'VE CALCULATED THE RATE OF OUR COLLAPSE AND THE RESULTING MOMENTUM!
THERE MAY BE A WAY TO, AS ELI'S DAD SAID, TURN THIS HANDICAP TO AN ADVANTAGE!
EVERYONE, FOLLOW BILLY'S LEAD!
LEAN FORWARD FORTY-THREE POINT SIX DEGREES!
DOES IT HAVE TO BE POINT SIX?
YES, KIM, IT DOES! AND IT HAS TO BE--
NOW!
WHOOOM
ZOOOOM

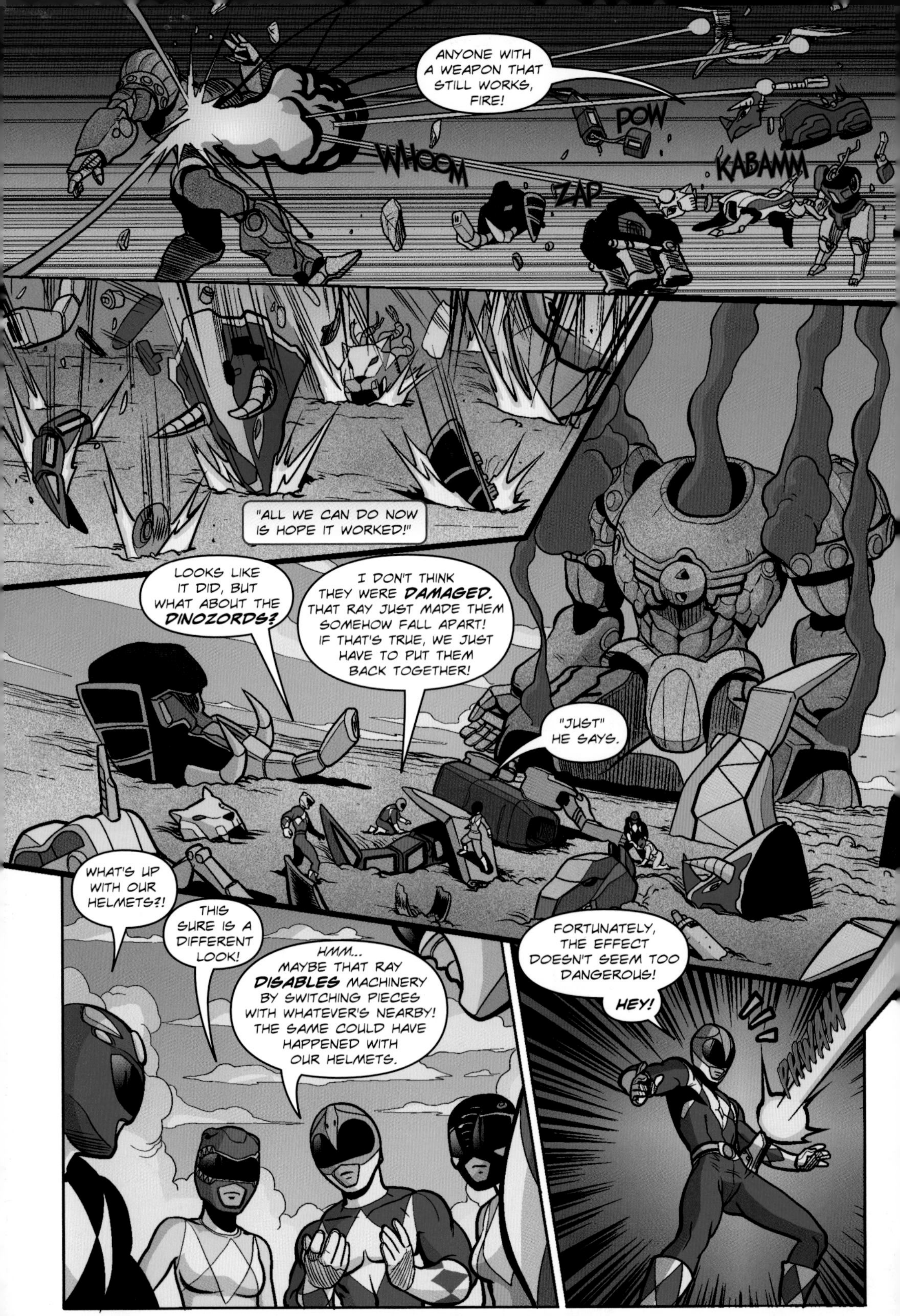
ANYONE WITH A WEAPON THAT STILL WORKS, FIRE!
POW
WHOOM
ZAP
KABAMM
"ALL WE CAN DO NOW IS HOPE IT WORKED!"
LOOKS LIKE IT DID, BUT WHAT ABOUT THE DINOZORDS?
I DON'T THINK THEY WERE DAMAGED. THAT RAY JUST MADE THEM SOMEHOW FALL APART! IF THAT'S TRUE, WE JUST HAVE TO PUT THEM BACK TOGETHER!
"JUST" HE SAYS.
WHAT'S UP WITH OUR HELMETS?!
THIS SURE IS A DIFFERENT LOOK!
HMM... MAYBE THAT RAY DISABLES MACHINERY BY SWITCHING PIECES WITH WHATEVER'S NEARBY! THE SAME COULD HAVE HAPPENED WITH OUR HELMETS.
FORTUNATELY, THE EFFECT DOESN'T SEEM TOO DANGEROUS!
HEY!

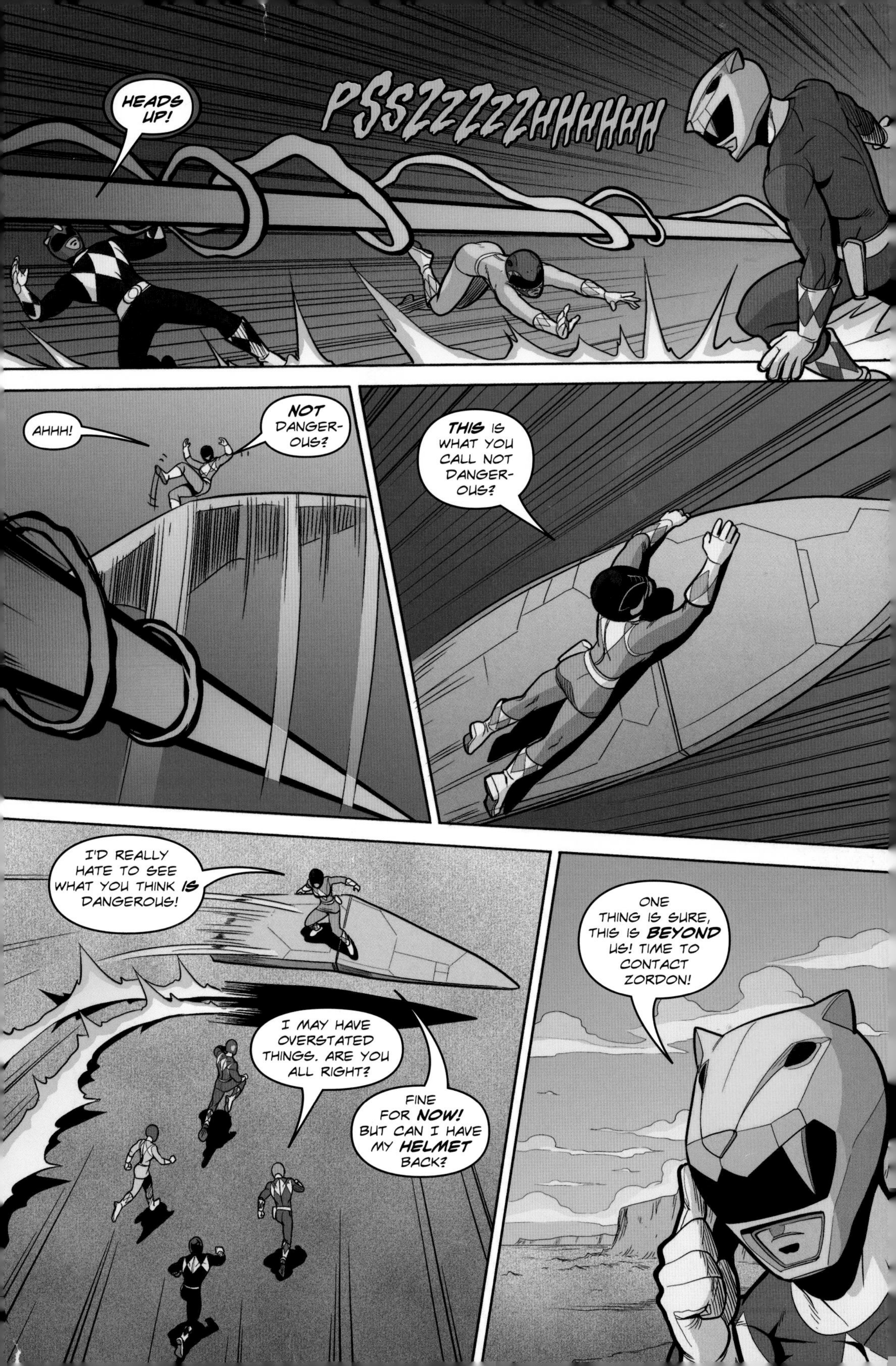
HEADS UP!
PSSZZZZZZHHHHHH
AHHH!
NOT DANGER-OUS?
THIS IS WHAT YOU CALL NOT DANGER-OUS?
I'D REALLY HATE TO SEE WHAT YOU THINK IS DANGEROUS!
I MAY HAVE OVERSTATED THINGS. ARE YOU ALL RIGHT?
FINE FOR NOW! BUT CAN I HAVE MY HELMET BACK?
ONE THING IS SURE, THIS IS BEYOND US! TIME TO CONTACT ZORDON!

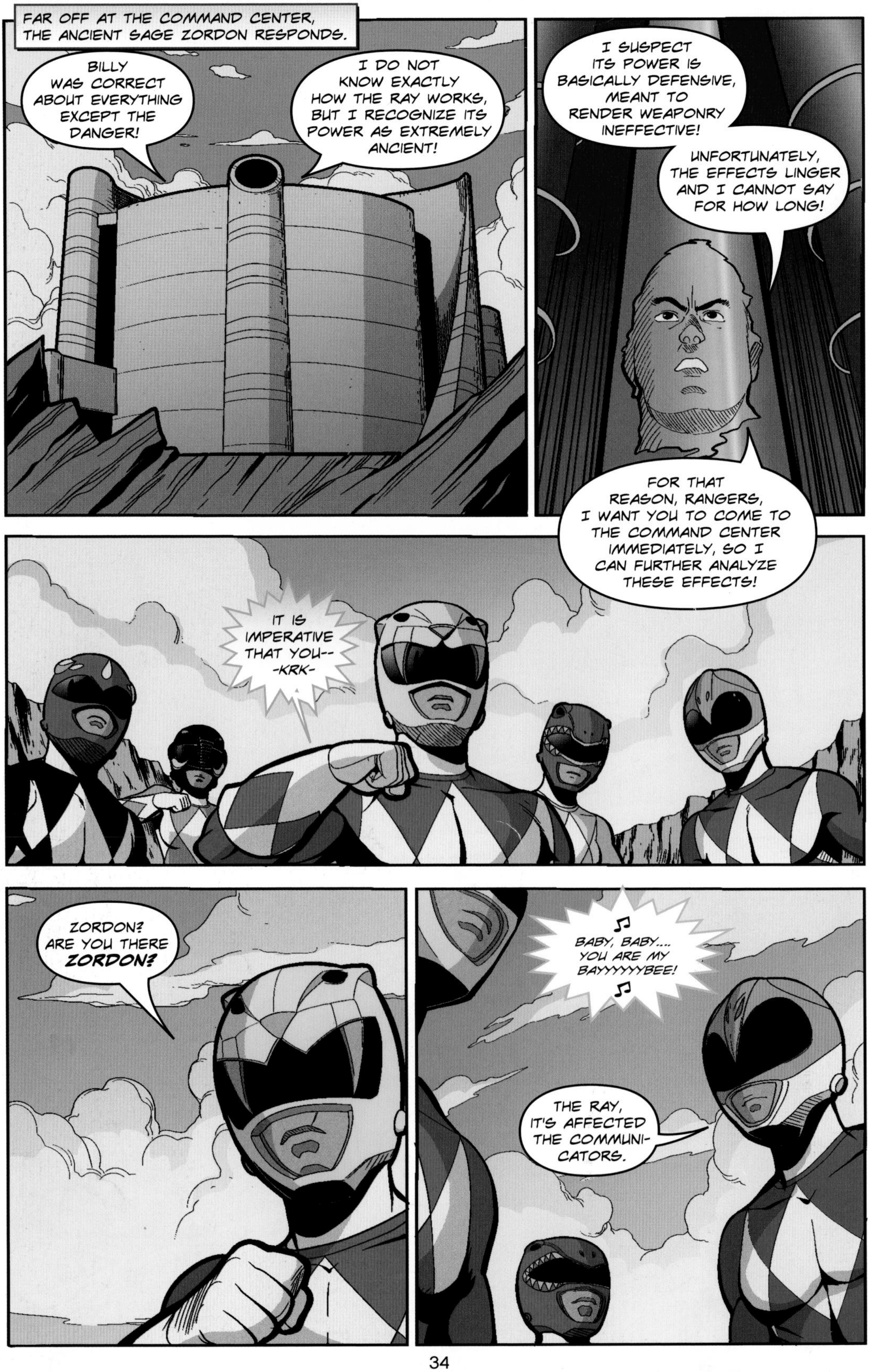
FAR OFF AT THE COMMAND CENTER, THE ANCIENT SAGE ZORDON RESPONDS.
BILLY WAS CORRECT ABOUT EVERYTHING EXCEPT THE DANGER!
I DO NOT KNOW EXACTLY HOW THE RAY WORKS, BUT I RECOGNIZE ITS POWER AS EXTREMELY ANCIENT!
I SUSPECT ITS POWER IS BASICALLY DEFENSIVE, MEANT TO RENDER WEAPONRY INEFFECTIVE!
UNFORTUNATELY, THE EFFECTS LINGER AND I CANNOT SAY FOR HOW LONG!
FOR THAT REASON, RANGERS, I WANT YOU TO COME TO THE COMMAND CENTER IMMEDIATELY, SO I CAN FURTHER ANALYZE THESE EFFECTS!
IT IS IMPERATIVE THAT YOU-- -KRK-
ZORDON? ARE YOU THERE ZORDON?
♫ BABY, BABY.... YOU ARE MY BAYYYYYYBEE! ♫
THE RAY, IT'S AFFECTED THE COMMUNI-CATORS.

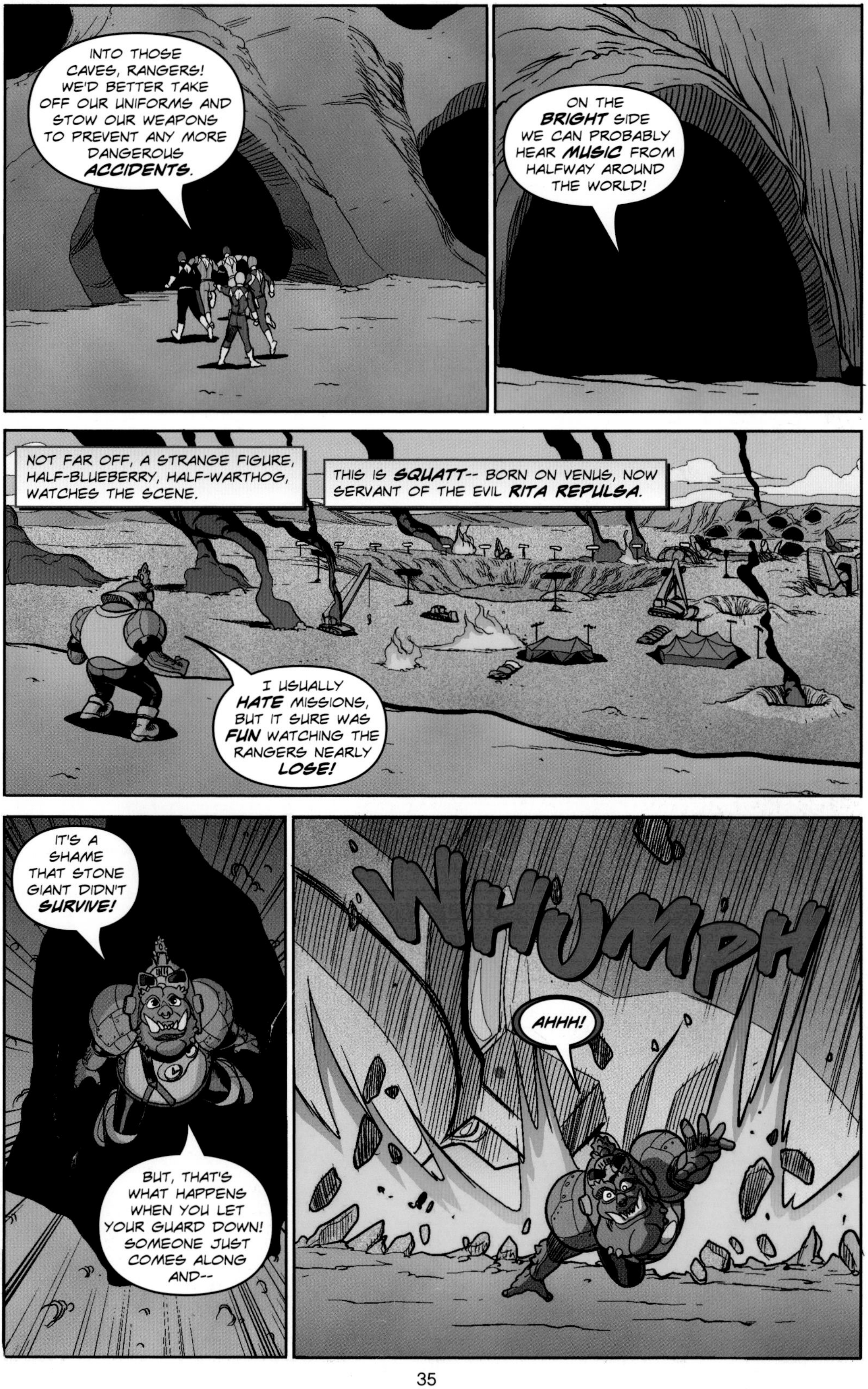
INTO THOSE CAVES, RANGERS! WE'D BETTER TAKE OFF OUR UNIFORMS AND STOW OUR WEAPONS TO PREVENT ANY MORE DANGEROUS ACCIDENTS.
ON THE BRIGHT SIDE WE CAN PROBABLY HEAR MUSIC FROM HALFWAY AROUND THE WORLD!
NOT FAR OFF, A STRANGE FIGURE, HALF-BLUEBERRY, HALF-WARTHOG, WATCHES THE SCENE.
THIS IS SQUATT-- BORN ON VENUS, NOW SERVANT OF THE EVIL RITA REPULSA.
I USUALLY HATE MISSIONS, BUT IT SURE WAS FUN WATCHING THE RANGERS NEARLY LOSE!
IT'S A SHAME THAT STONE GIANT DIDN'T SURVIVE!
BUT, THAT'S WHAT HAPPENS WHEN YOU LET YOUR GUARD DOWN! SOMEONE JUST COMES ALONG AND--
WHUMPH
AHHH!

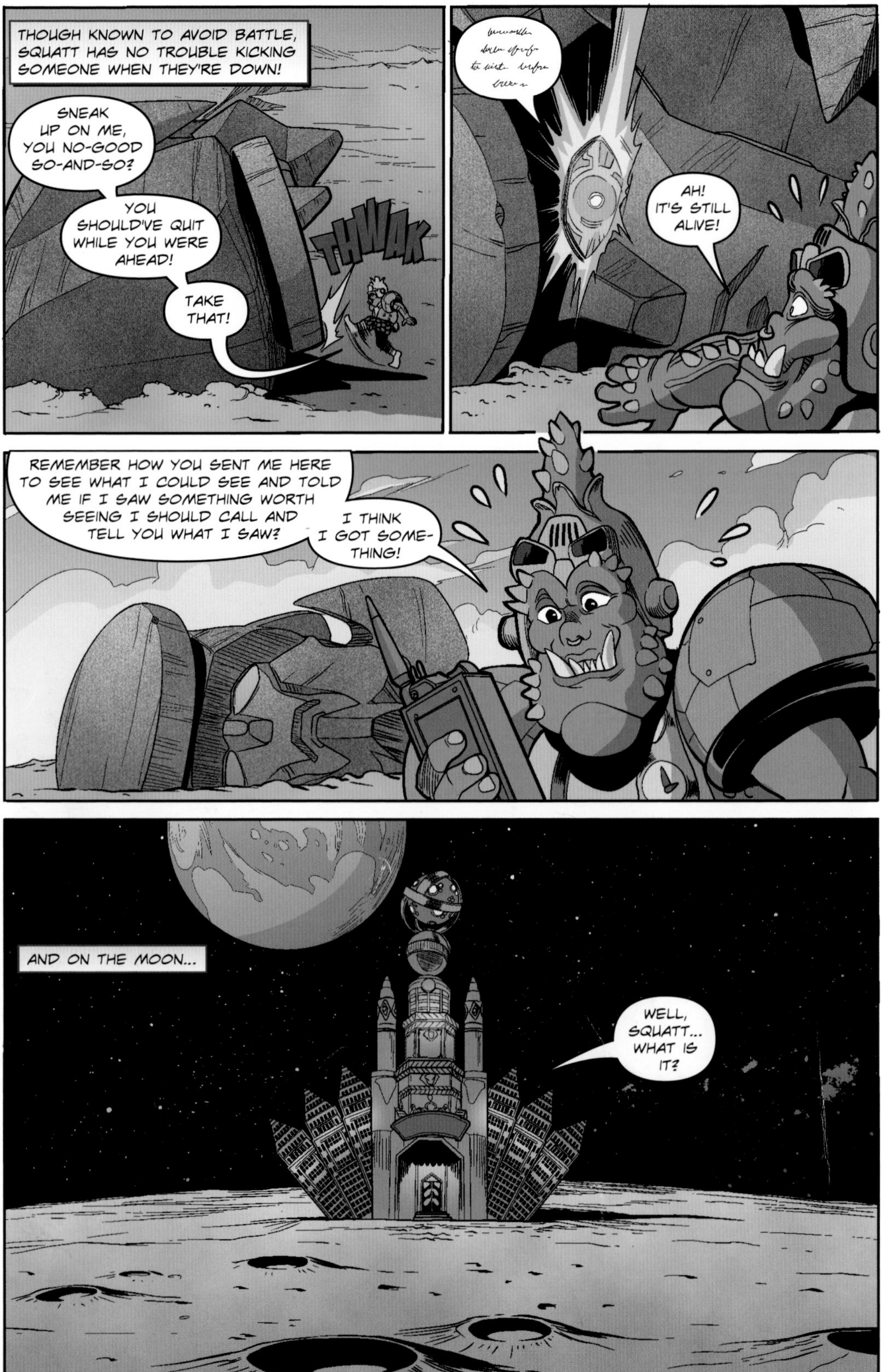
THOUGH KNOWN TO AVOID BATTLE, SQUATT HAS NO TROUBLE KICKING SOMEONE WHEN THEY'RE DOWN!
SNEAK UP ON ME, YOU NO-GOOD SO-AND-SO?
YOU SHOULD'VE QUIT WHILE YOU WERE AHEAD!
THWAK
TAKE THAT!
AH! IT'S STILL ALIVE!
REMEMBER HOW YOU SENT ME HERE TO SEE WHAT I COULD SEE AND TOLD ME IF I SAW SOMETHING WORTH SEEING I SHOULD CALL AND TELL YOU WHAT I SAW?
I THINK I GOT SOME-THING!
AND ON THE MOON...
WELL, SQUATT... WHAT IS IT?

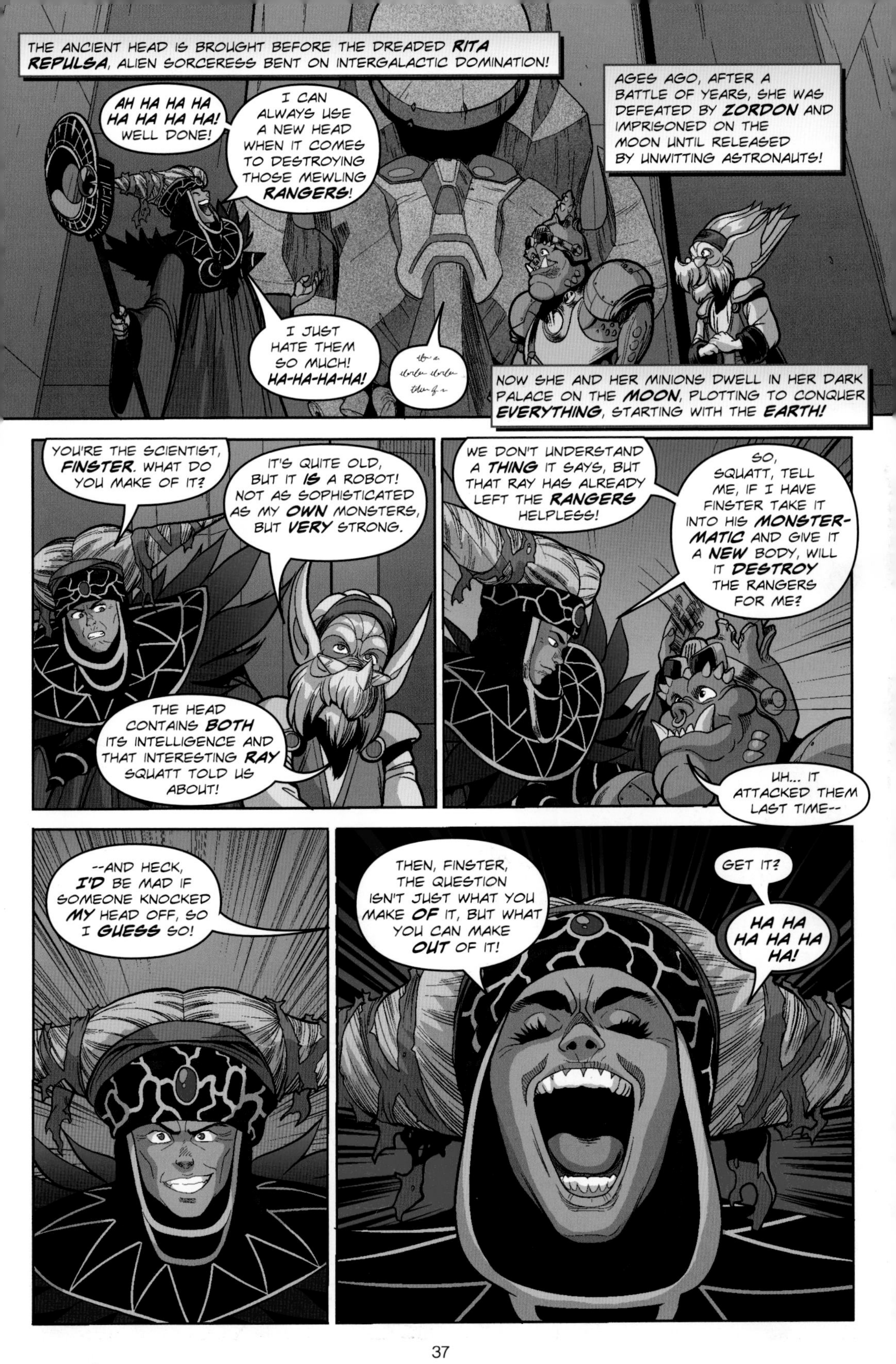
THE ANCIENT HEAD IS BROUGHT BEFORE THE DREADED RITA REPULSA, ALIEN SORCERESS BENT ON INTERGALACTIC DOMINATION!
AGES AGO, AFTER A BATTLE OF YEARS, SHE WAS DEFEATED BY ZORDON AND IMPRISONED ON THE MOON UNTIL RELEASED BY UNWITTING ASTRONAUTS!
AH HA HA HA HA HA HA HA! WELL DONE!
I CAN ALWAYS USE A NEW HEAD WHEN IT COMES TO DESTROYING THOSE MEWLING RANGERS!
I JUST HATE THEM SO MUCH! HA-HA-HA-HA!
NOW SHE AND HER MINIONS DWELL IN HER DARK PALACE ON THE MOON, PLOTTING TO CONQUER EVERYTHING, STARTING WITH THE EARTH!
YOU'RE THE SCIENTIST, FINSTER. WHAT DO YOU MAKE OF IT?
IT'S QUITE OLD, BUT IT IS A ROBOT! NOT AS SOPHISTICATED AS MY OWN MONSTERS, BUT VERY STRONG.
THE HEAD CONTAINS BOTH ITS INTELLIGENCE AND THAT INTERESTING RAY SQUATT TOLD US ABOUT!
WE DON'T UNDERSTAND A THING IT SAYS, BUT THAT RAY HAS ALREADY LEFT THE RANGERS HELPLESS!
SO, SQUATT, TELL ME, IF I HAVE FINSTER TAKE IT INTO HIS MONSTER-MATIC AND GIVE IT A NEW BODY, WILL IT DESTROY THE RANGERS FOR ME?
UH... IT ATTACKED THEM LAST TIME--
--AND HECK, I'D BE MAD IF SOMEONE KNOCKED MY HEAD OFF, SO I GUESS SO!
THEN, FINSTER, THE QUESTION ISN'T JUST WHAT YOU MAKE OF IT, BUT WHAT YOU CAN MAKE OUT OF IT!
GET IT?
HA HA HA HA HA HA!

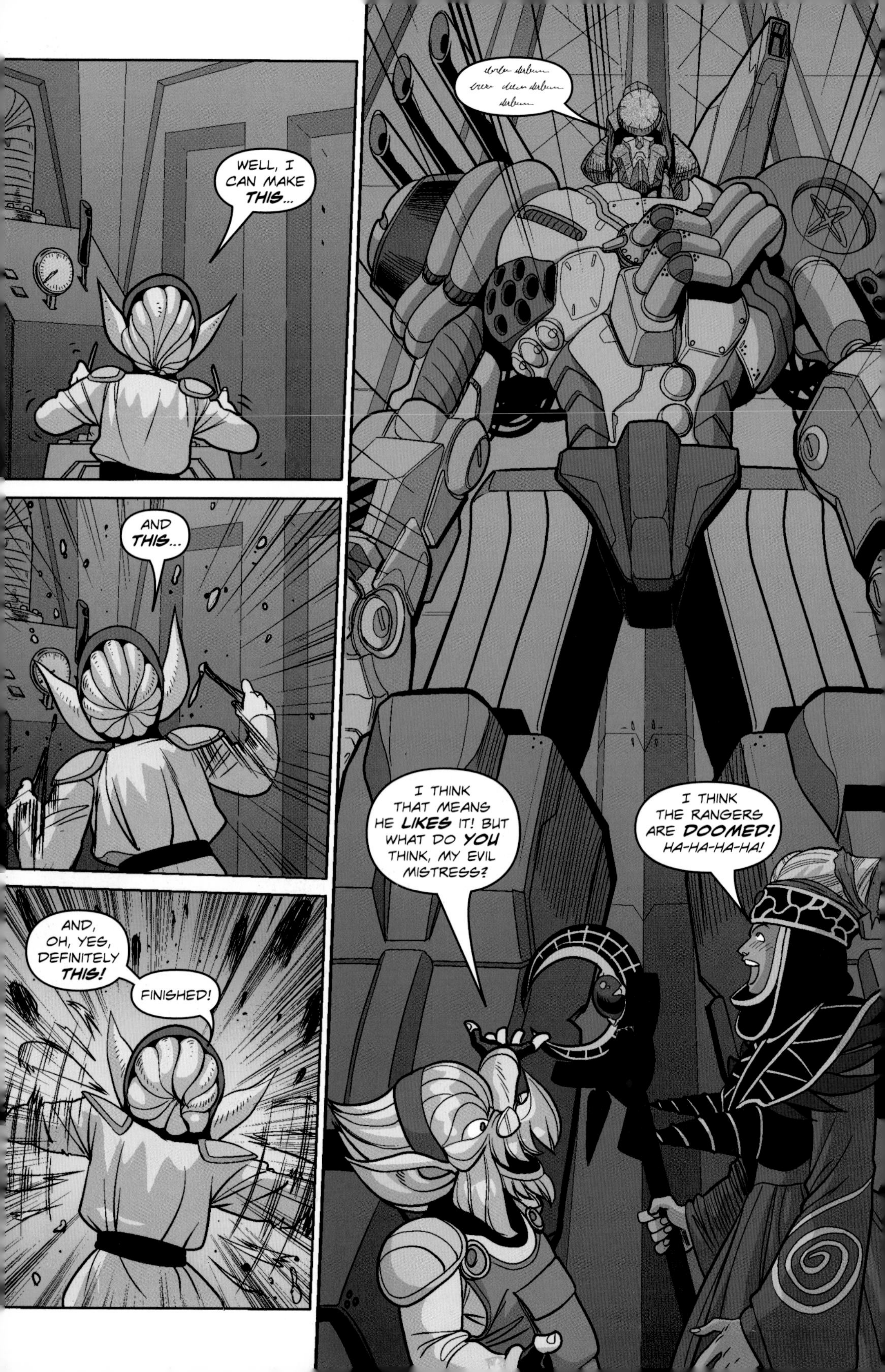
WELL, I CAN MAKE THIS...
AND THIS...
AND, OH, YES, DEFINITELY THIS!
FINISHED!
I THINK THAT MEANS HE LIKES IT! BUT WHAT DO YOU THINK, MY EVIL MISTRESS?
I THINK THE RANGERS ARE DOOMED! HA-HA-HA-HA!

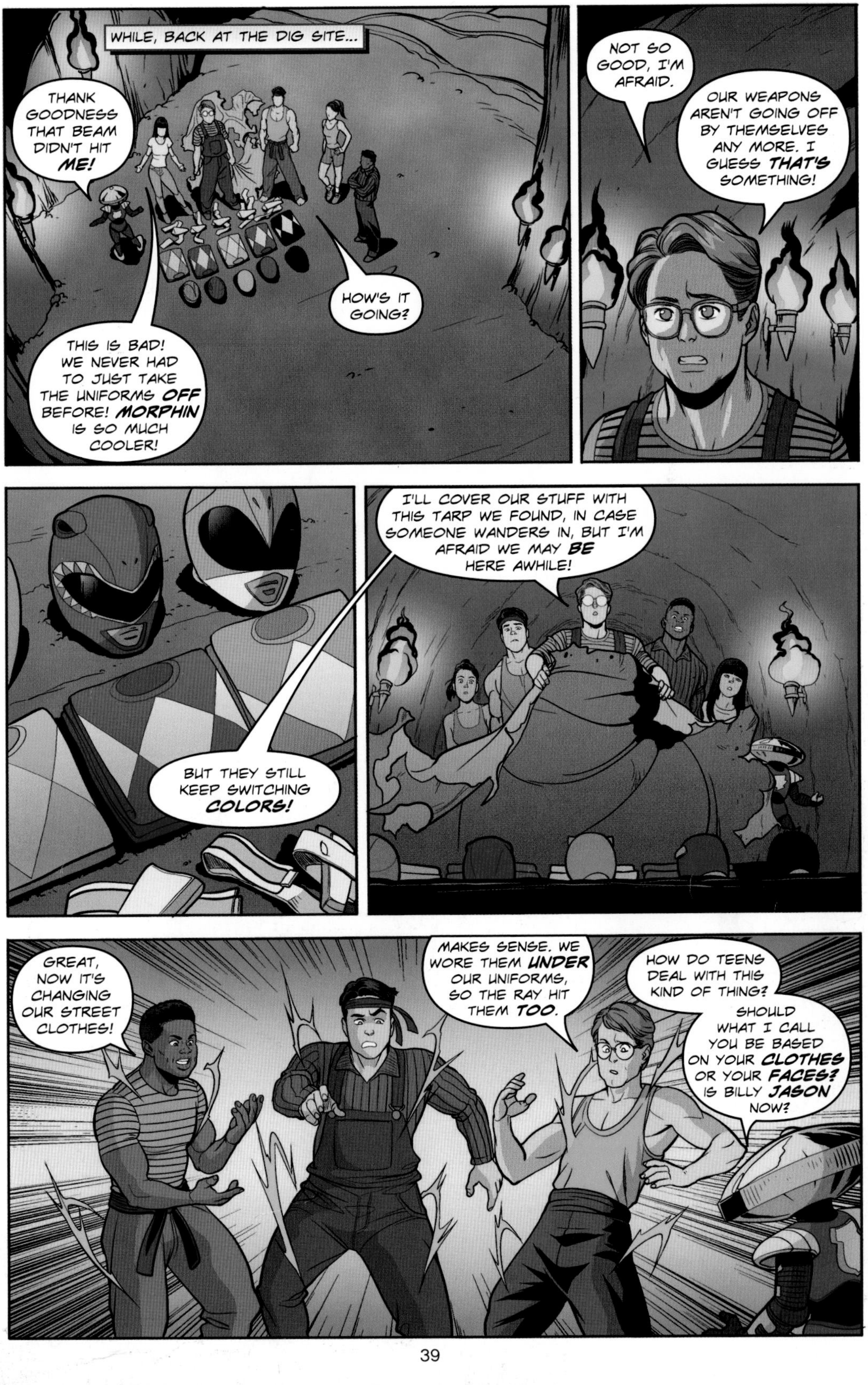
WHILE, BACK AT THE DIG SITE...
THANK GOODNESS THAT BEAM DIDN'T HIT ME!
THIS IS BAD! WE NEVER HAD TO JUST TAKE THE UNIFORMS OFF BEFORE! MORPHIN IS SO MUCH COOLER!
HOW'S IT GOING?
NOT SO GOOD, I'M AFRAID.
OUR WEAPONS AREN'T GOING OFF BY THEMSELVES ANY MORE. I GUESS THAT'S SOMETHING!
BUT THEY STILL KEEP SWITCHING COLORS!
I'LL COVER OUR STUFF WITH THIS TARP WE FOUND, IN CASE SOMEONE WANDERS IN, BUT I'M AFRAID WE MAY BE HERE AWHILE!
GREAT, NOW IT'S CHANGING OUR STREET CLOTHES!
MAKES SENSE. WE WORE THEM UNDER OUR UNIFORMS, SO THE RAY HIT THEM TOO.
HOW DO TEENS DEAL WITH THIS KIND OF THING?
SHOULD WHAT I CALL YOU BE BASED ON YOUR CLOTHES OR YOUR FACES? IS BILLY JASON NOW?

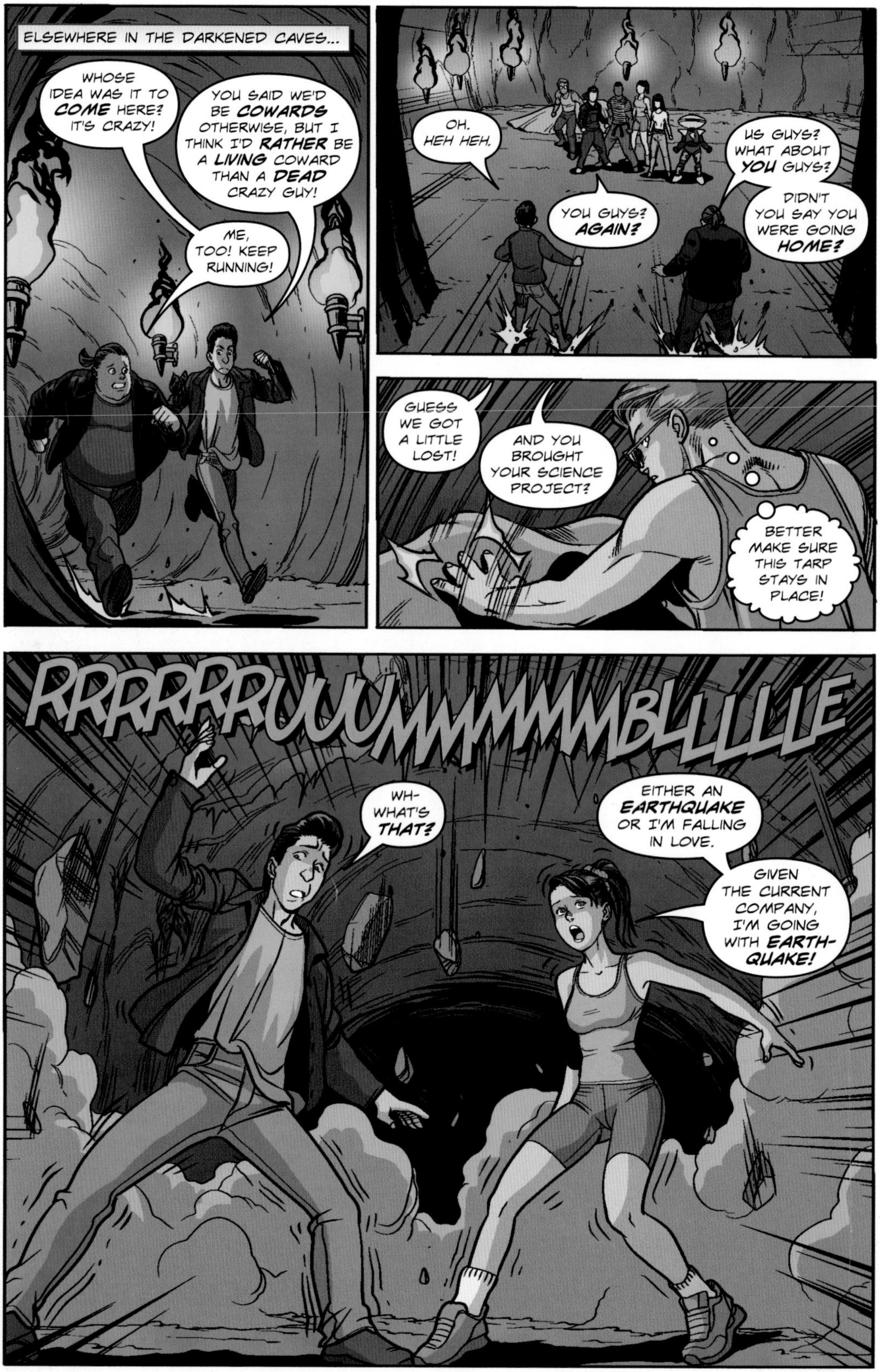
ELSEWHERE IN THE DARKENED CAVES...
WHOSE IDEA WAS IT TO COME HERE? IT'S CRAZY!
YOU SAID WE'D BE COWARDS OTHERWISE, BUT I THINK I'D RATHER BE A LIVING COWARD THAN A DEAD CRAZY GUY!
ME, TOO! KEEP RUNNING!
OH. HEH HEH.
YOU GUYS? AGAIN?
US GUYS? WHAT ABOUT YOU GUYS?
DIDN'T YOU SAY YOU WERE GOING HOME?
GUESS WE GOT A LITTLE LOST!
AND YOU BROUGHT YOUR SCIENCE PROJECT?
BETTER MAKE SURE THIS TARP STAYS IN PLACE!
RRRRRRUUUMMMMMMBLLLLLE
WH-WHAT'S THAT?
EITHER AN EARTHQUAKE OR I'M FALLING IN LOVE.
GIVEN THE CURRENT COMPANY, I'M GOING WITH EARTH-QUAKE!

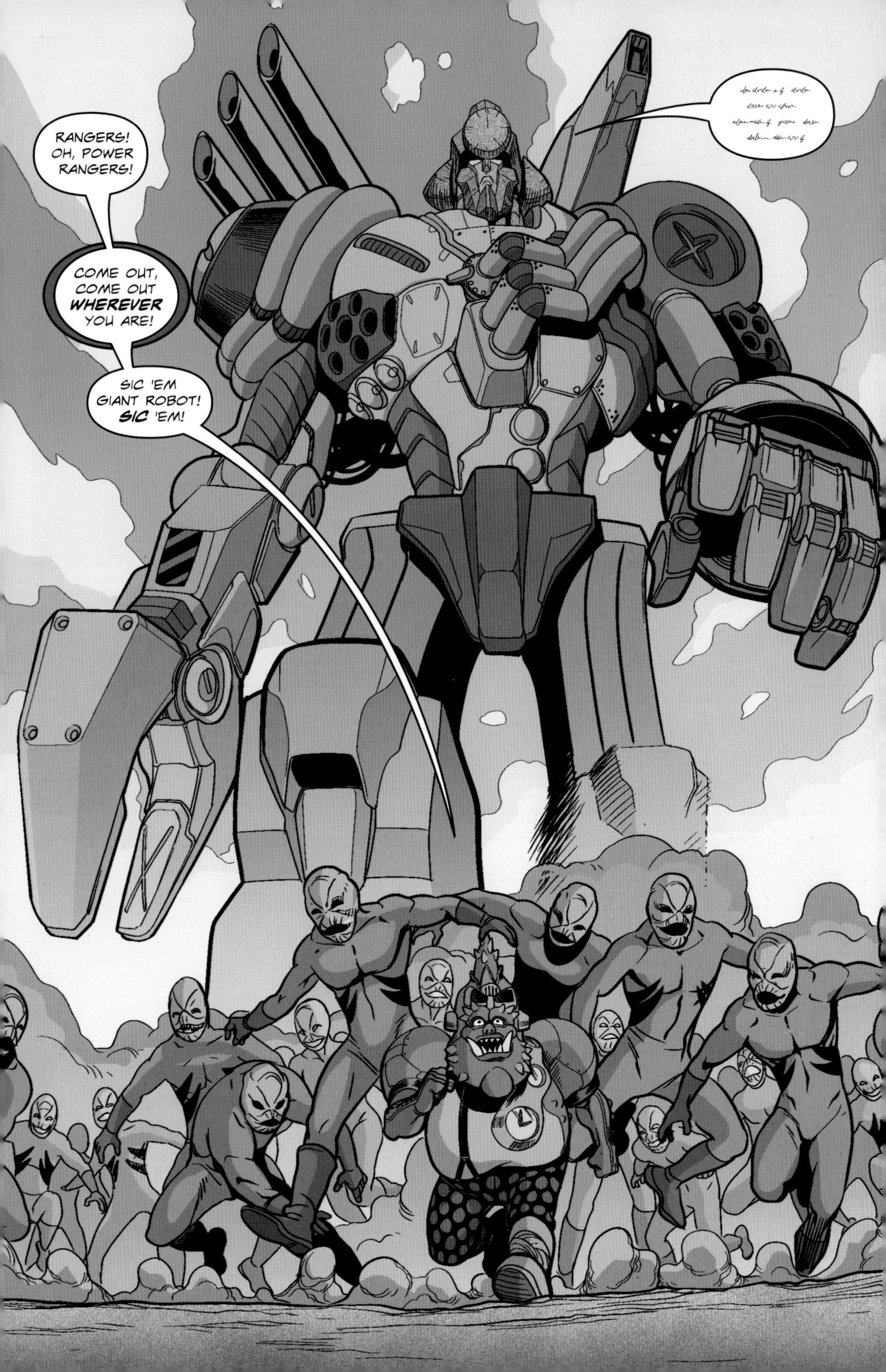
RANGERS! OH, POWER RANGERS!
COME OUT, COME OUT ***WHEREVER*** YOU ARE!
SIC 'EM GIANT ROBOT! ***SIC*** 'EM!

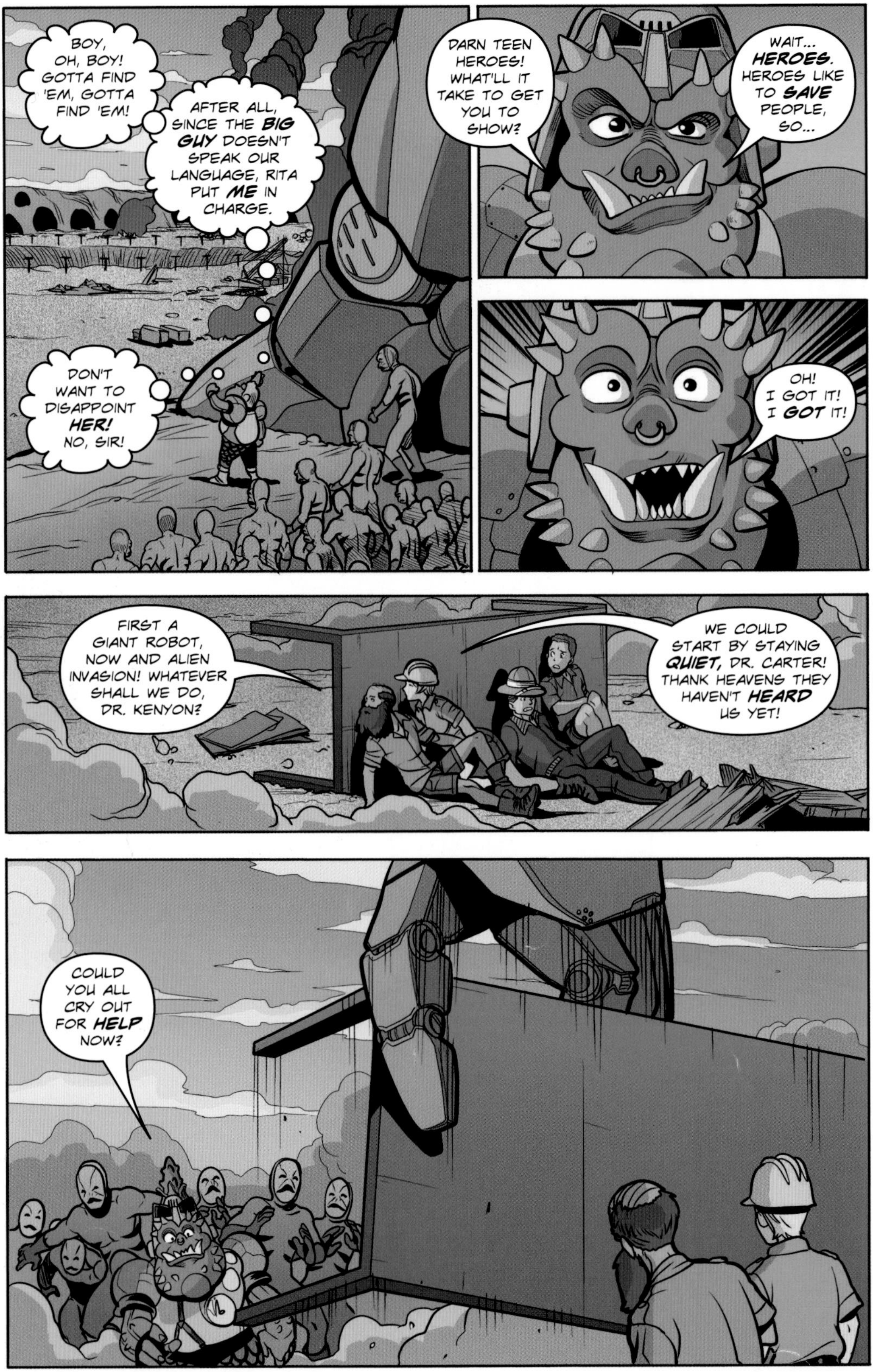
BOY, OH, BOY! GOTTA FIND 'EM, GOTTA FIND 'EM!
AFTER ALL, SINCE THE BIG GUY DOESN'T SPEAK OUR LANGUAGE, RITA PUT ME IN CHARGE.
DON'T WANT TO DISAPPOINT HER! NO, SIR!
DARN TEEN HEROES! WHAT'LL IT TAKE TO GET YOU TO SHOW?
WAIT... HEROES. HEROES LIKE TO SAVE PEOPLE, SO...
OH! I GOT IT! I GOT IT!
FIRST A GIANT ROBOT, NOW AND ALIEN INVASION! WHATEVER SHALL WE DO, DR. KENYON?
WE COULD START BY STAYING QUIET, DR. CARTER! THANK HEAVENS THEY HAVEN'T HEARD US YET!
COULD YOU ALL CRY OUT FOR HELP NOW?

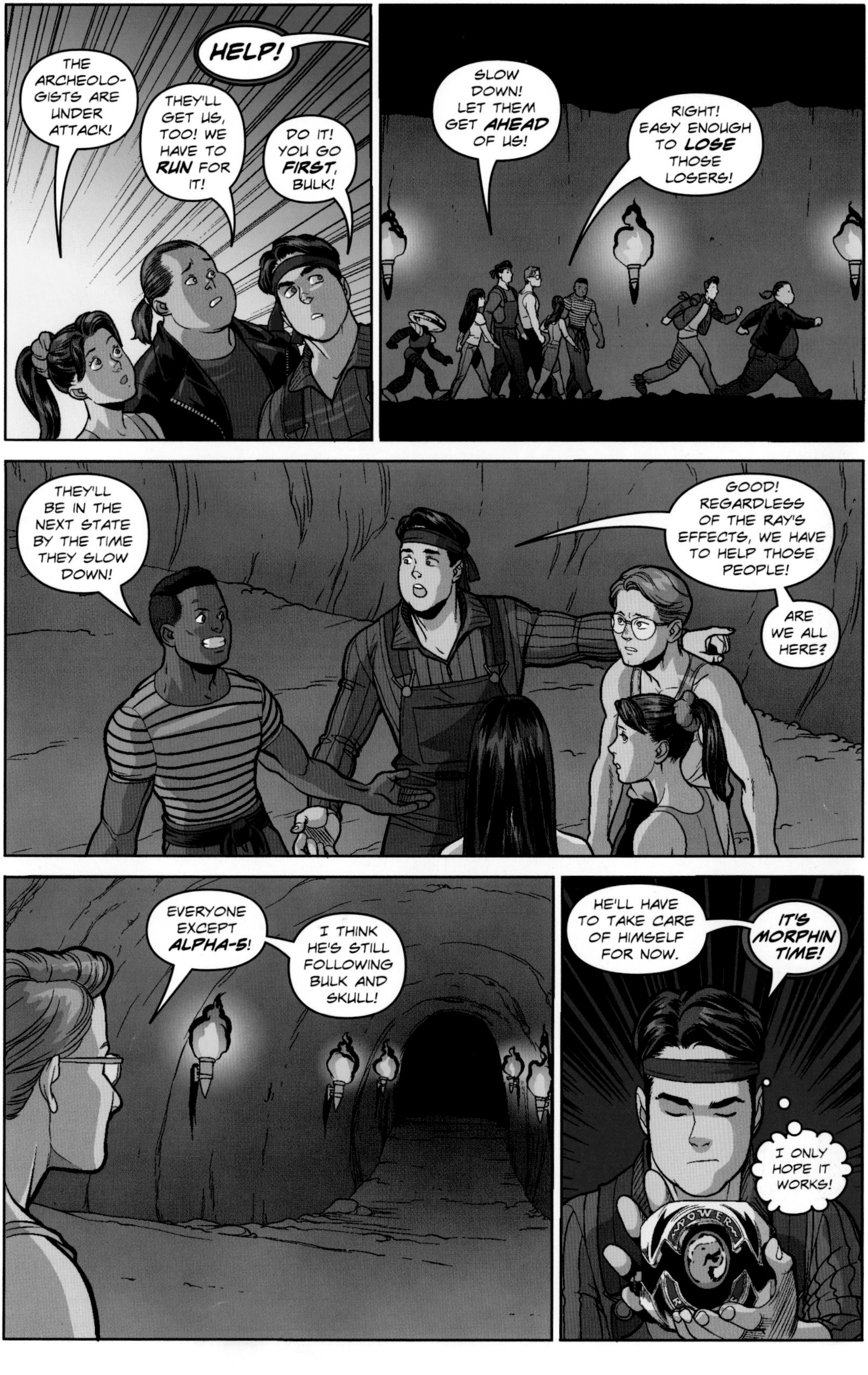

THE ARCHEOLOGISTS ARE UNDER ATTACK!
HELP!
THEY'LL GET US, TOO! WE HAVE TO RUN FOR IT!
DO IT! YOU GO FIRST, BULK!
SLOW DOWN! LET THEM GET AHEAD OF US!
RIGHT! EASY ENOUGH TO LOSE THOSE LOSERS!
THEY'LL BE IN THE NEXT STATE BY THE TIME THEY SLOW DOWN!
GOOD! REGARDLESS OF THE RAY'S EFFECTS, WE HAVE TO HELP THOSE PEOPLE!
ARE WE ALL HERE?
EVERYONE EXCEPT ALPHA-5!
I THINK HE'S STILL FOLLOWING BULK AND SKULL!
HE'LL HAVE TO TAKE CARE OF HIMSELF FOR NOW.
IT'S MORPHIN TIME!
I ONLY HOPE IT WORKS!
POWER

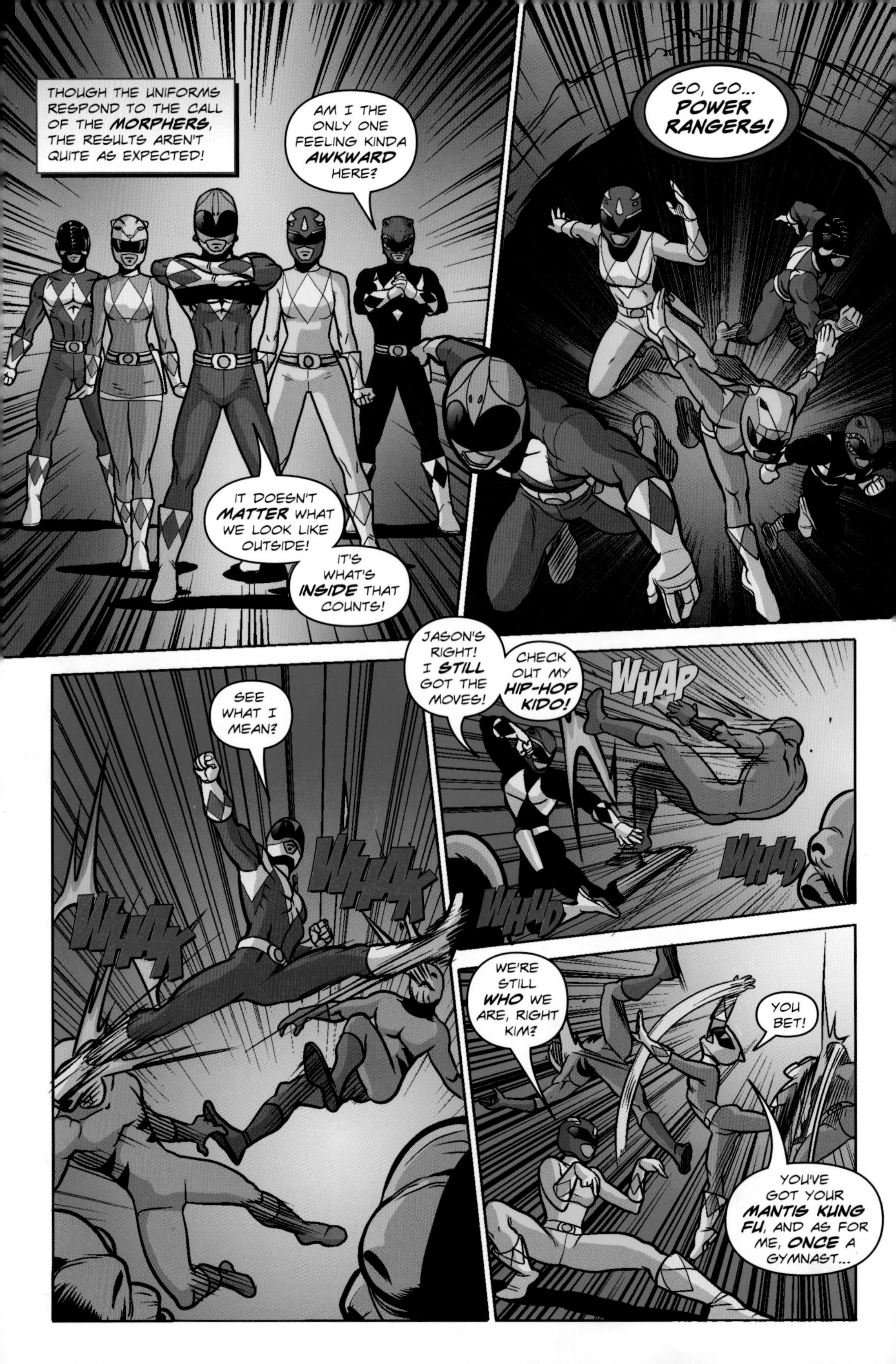
THOUGH THE UNIFORMS RESPOND TO THE CALL OF THE MORPHERS, THE RESULTS AREN'T QUITE AS EXPECTED!
AM I THE ONLY ONE FEELING KINDA AWKWARD HERE?
IT DOESN'T MATTER WHAT WE LOOK LIKE OUTSIDE!
IT'S WHAT'S INSIDE THAT COUNTS!
GO, GO... POWER RANGERS!
SEE WHAT I MEAN?
WHAK
WHAK
JASON'S RIGHT! I STILL GOT THE MOVES!
CHECK OUT MY HIP-HOP KIDO!
WHAP
WHUD
WHUD
WE'RE STILL WHO WE ARE, RIGHT KIM?
YOU BET!
YOU'VE GOT YOUR MANTIS KUNG FU, AND AS FOR ME, ONCE A GYMNAST...

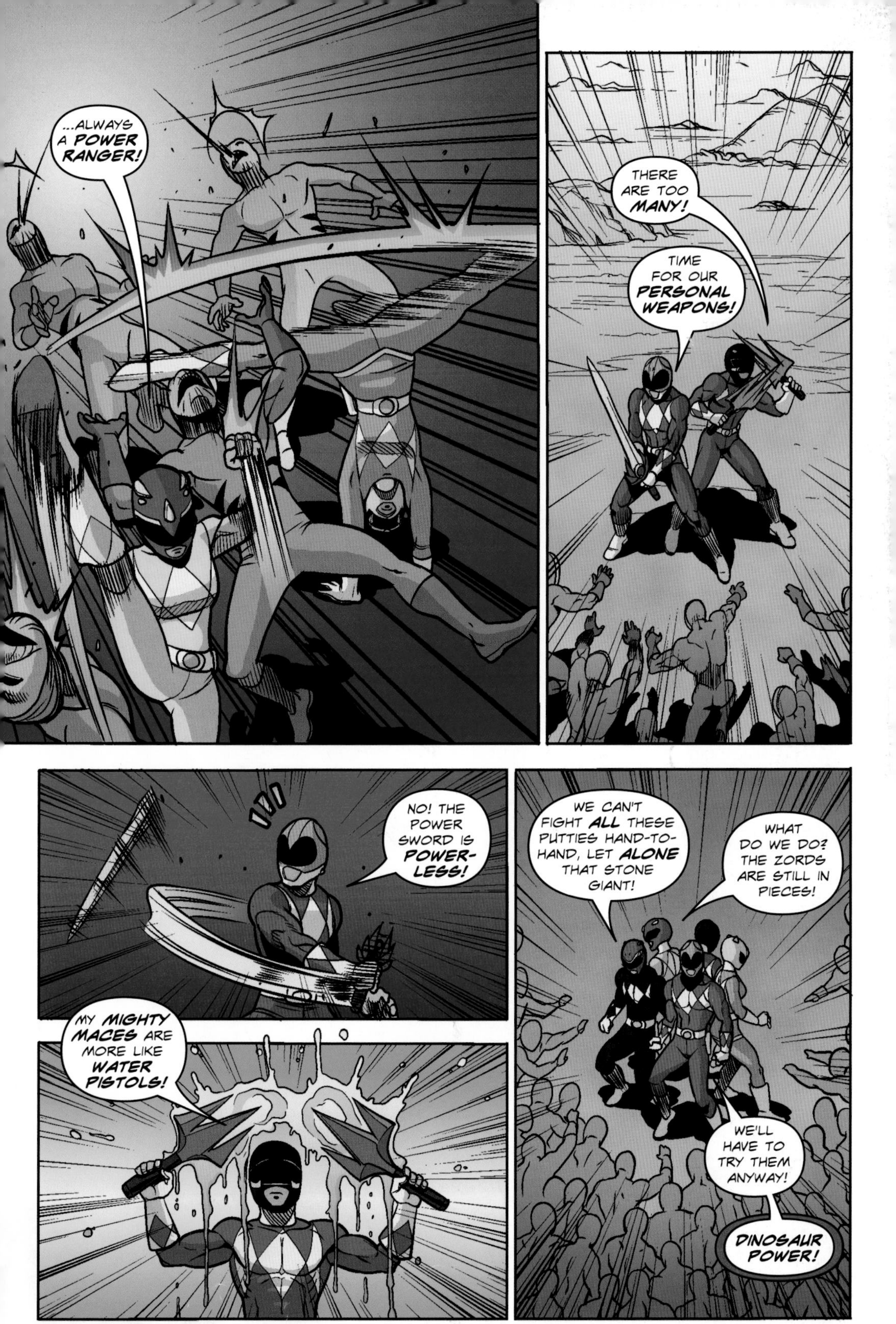
...ALWAYS A POWER RANGER!
THERE ARE TOO MANY!
TIME FOR OUR PERSONAL WEAPONS!
NO! THE POWER SWORD IS POWER-LESS!
MY MIGHTY MACES ARE MORE LIKE WATER PISTOLS!
WE CAN'T FIGHT ALL THESE PUTTIES HAND-TO-HAND, LET ALONE THAT STONE GIANT!
WHAT DO WE DO? THE ZORDS ARE STILL IN PIECES!
WE'LL HAVE TO TRY THEM ANYWAY!
DINOSAUR POWER!

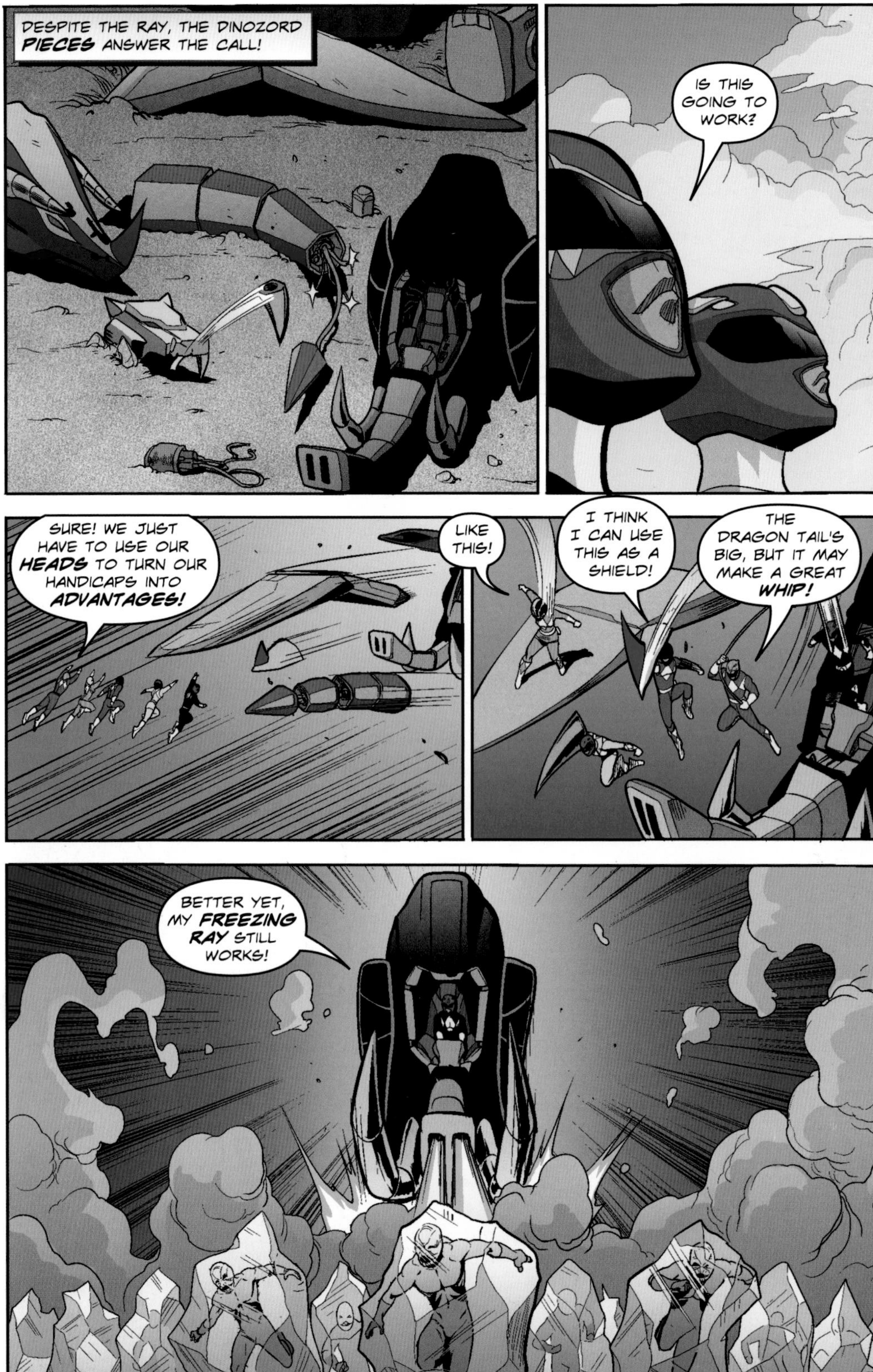
DESPITE THE RAY, THE DINOZORD PIECES ANSWER THE CALL!
IS THIS GOING TO WORK?
SURE! WE JUST HAVE TO USE OUR HEADS TO TURN OUR HANDICAPS INTO ADVANTAGES!
LIKE THIS!
I THINK I CAN USE THIS AS A SHIELD!
THE DRAGON TAIL'S BIG, BUT IT MAY MAKE A GREAT WHIP!
BETTER YET, MY FREEZING RAY STILL WORKS!

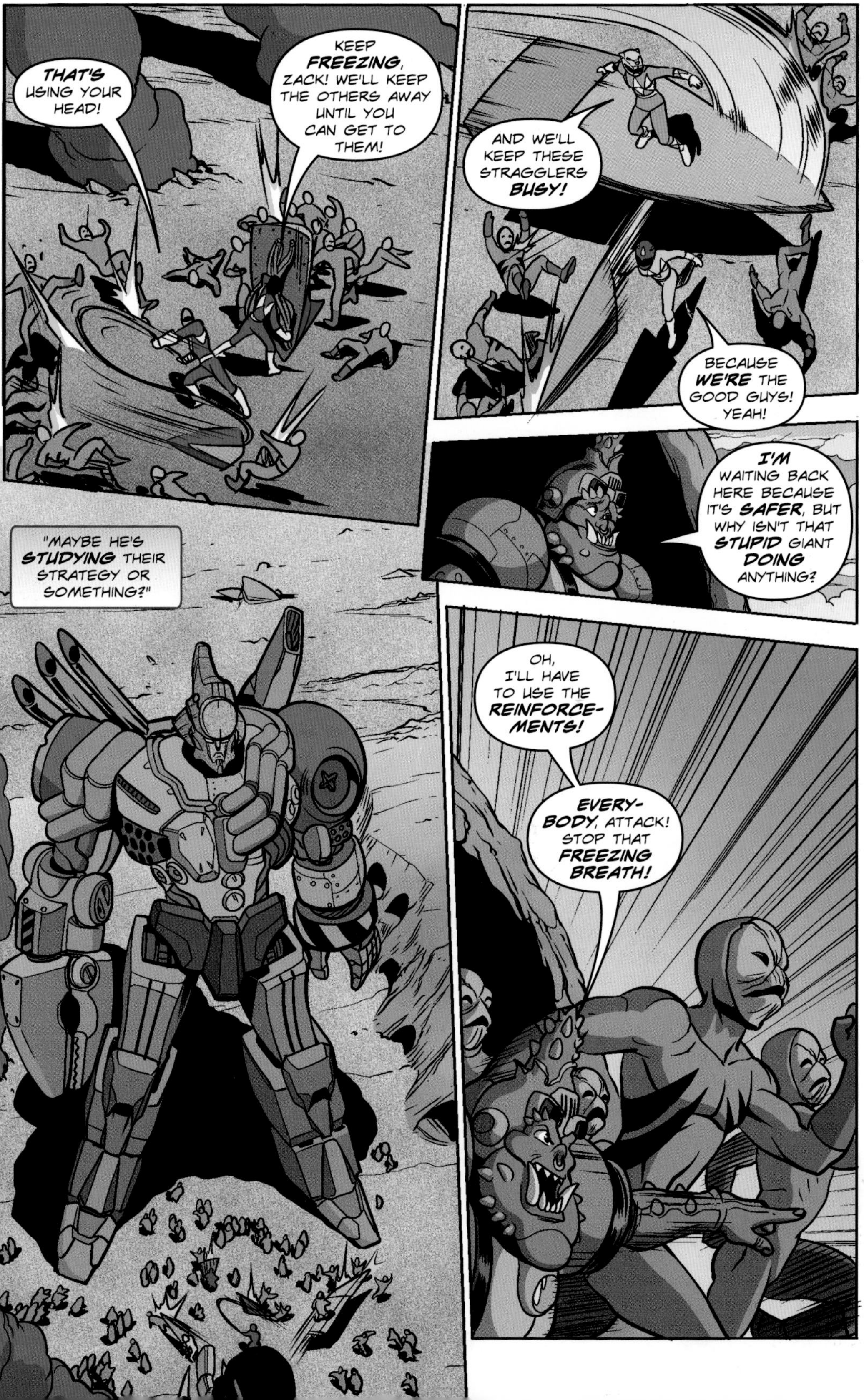
THAT'S USING YOUR HEAD!
KEEP FREEZING, ZACK! WE'LL KEEP THE OTHERS AWAY UNTIL YOU CAN GET TO THEM!
AND WE'LL KEEP THESE STRAGGLERS BUSY!
BECAUSE WE'RE THE GOOD GUYS! YEAH!
I'M WAITING BACK HERE BECAUSE IT'S SAFER, BUT WHY ISN'T THAT STUPID GIANT DOING ANYTHING?
"MAYBE HE'S STUDYING THEIR STRATEGY OR SOMETHING?"
OH, I'LL HAVE TO USE THE REINFORCE-MENTS!
EVERY-BODY, ATTACK! STOP THAT FREEZING BREATH!

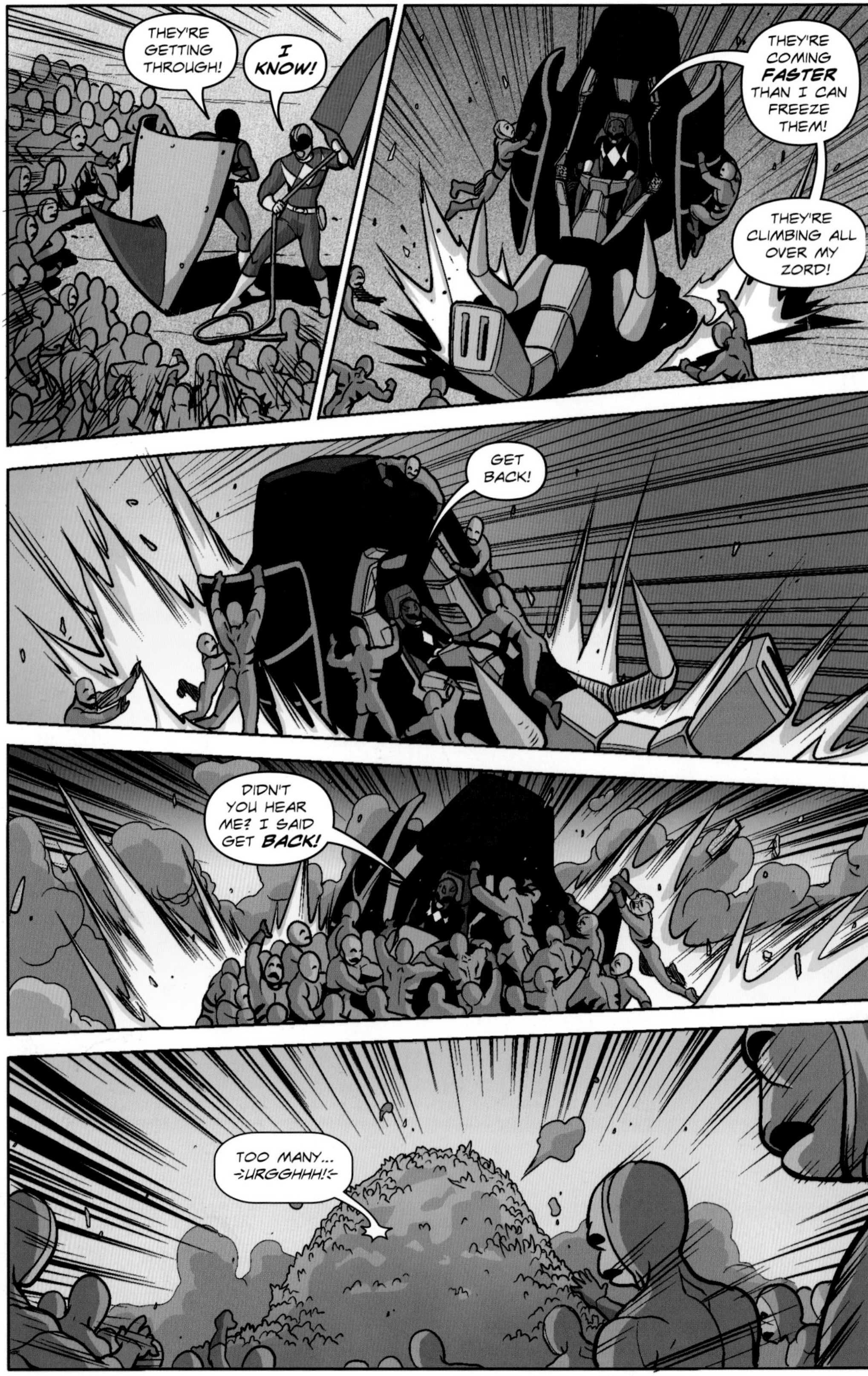
THEY'RE GETTING THROUGH!
I KNOW!
THEY'RE COMING FASTER THAN I CAN FREEZE THEM!
THEY'RE CLIMBING ALL OVER MY ZORD!
GET BACK!
DIDN'T YOU HEAR ME? I SAID GET BACK!
TOO MANY... URGGHHH!

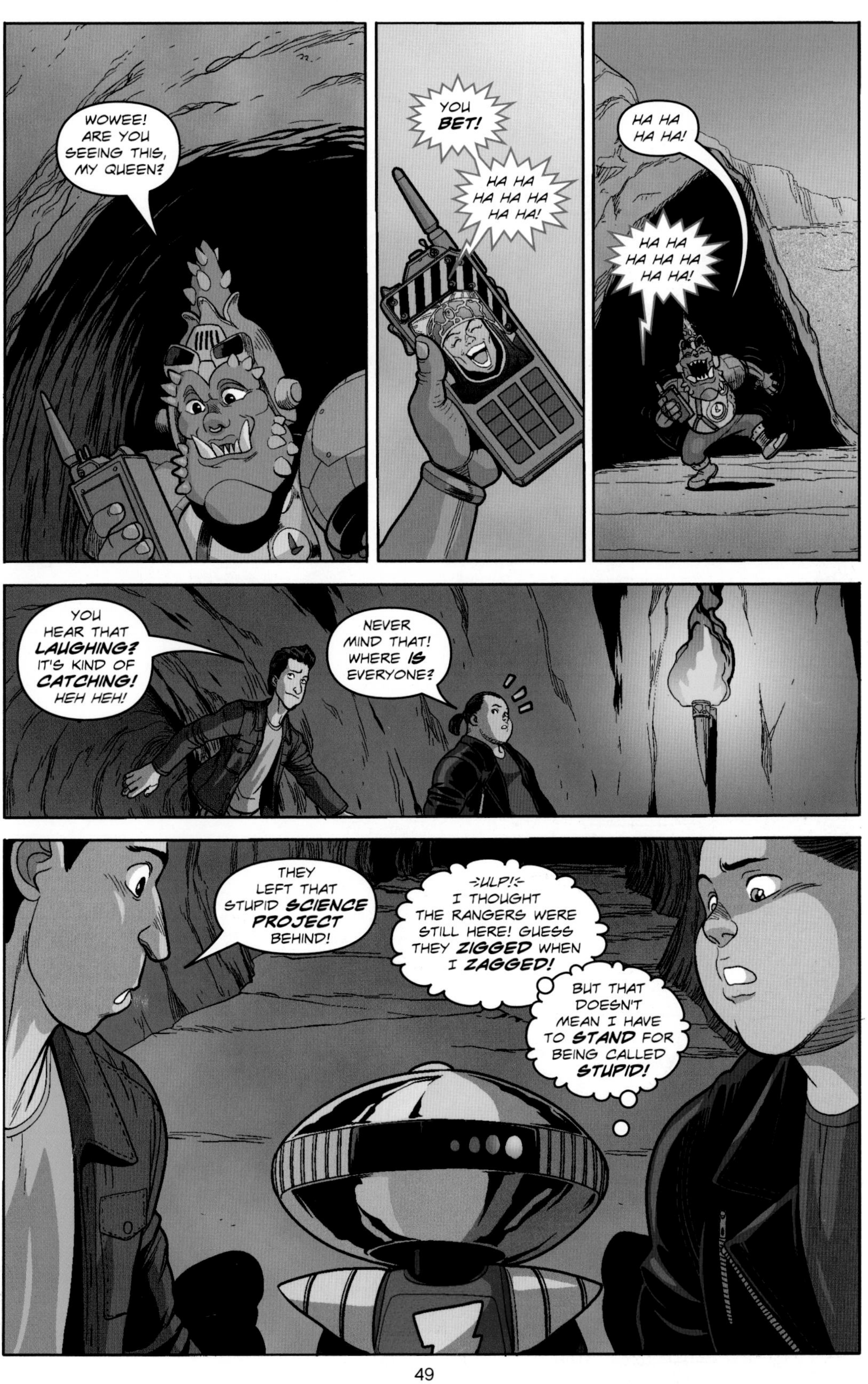
WOWEE! ARE YOU SEEING THIS, MY QUEEN?
YOU BET!
HA HA HA HA HA HA HA HA!
HA HA HA HA!
HA HA HA HA HA HA HA!
YOU HEAR THAT LAUGHING? IT'S KIND OF CATCHING! HEH HEH!
NEVER MIND THAT! WHERE IS EVERYONE?
THEY LEFT THAT STUPID SCIENCE PROJECT BEHIND!
-ULP!- I THOUGHT THE RANGERS WERE STILL HERE! GUESS THEY ZIGGED WHEN I ZAGGED!
BUT THAT DOESN'T MEAN I HAVE TO STAND FOR BEING CALLED STUPID!

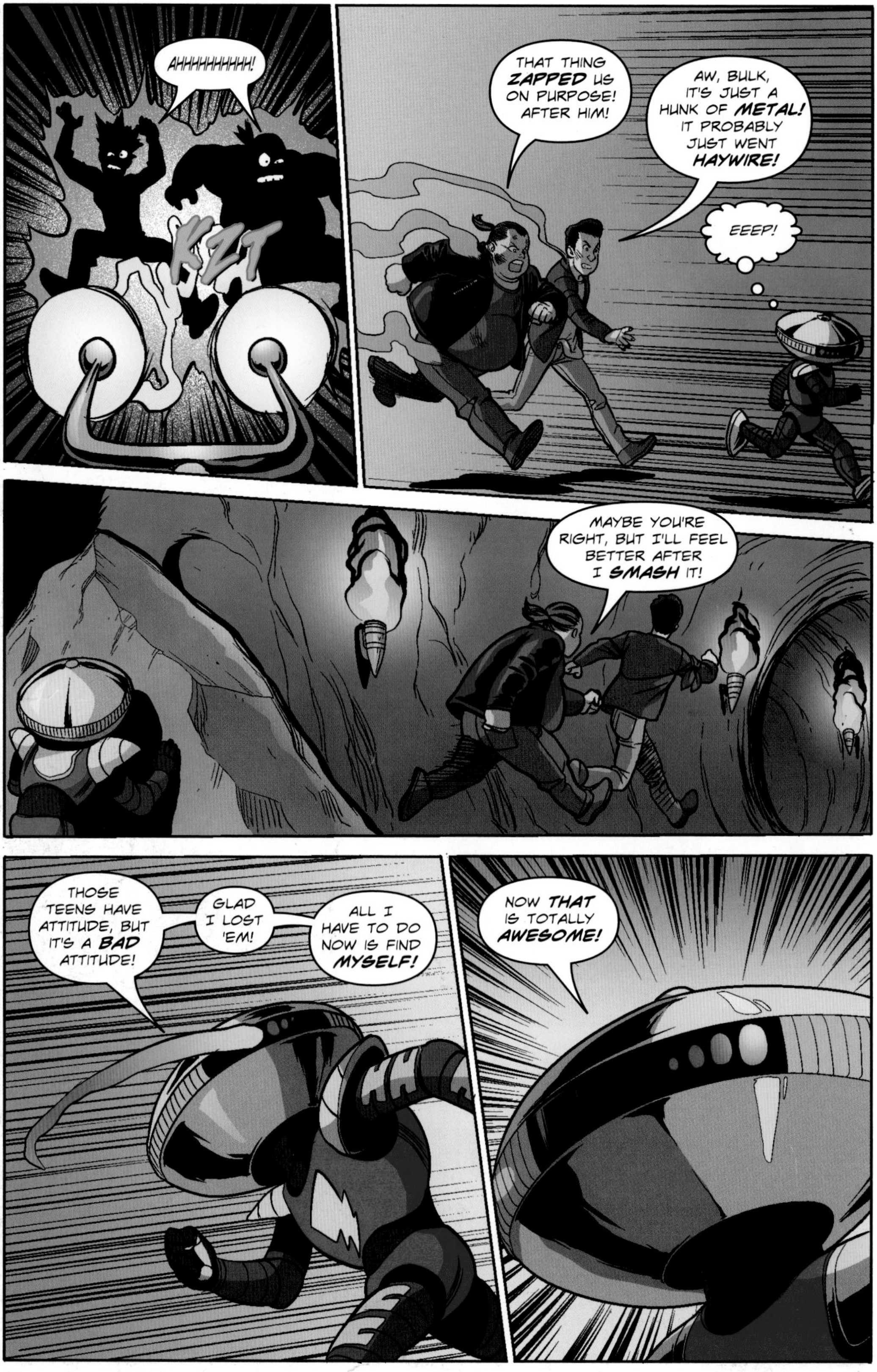
AHHHHHHHHHH!
KZT
THAT THING ZAPPED US ON PURPOSE! AFTER HIM!
AW, BULK, IT'S JUST A HUNK OF METAL! IT PROBABLY JUST WENT HAYWIRE!
EEEP!
MAYBE YOU'RE RIGHT, BUT I'LL FEEL BETTER AFTER I SMASH IT!
THOSE TEENS HAVE ATTITUDE, BUT IT'S A BAD ATTITUDE!
GLAD I LOST 'EM!
ALL I HAVE TO DO NOW IS FIND MYSELF!
NOW THAT IS TOTALLY AWESOME!

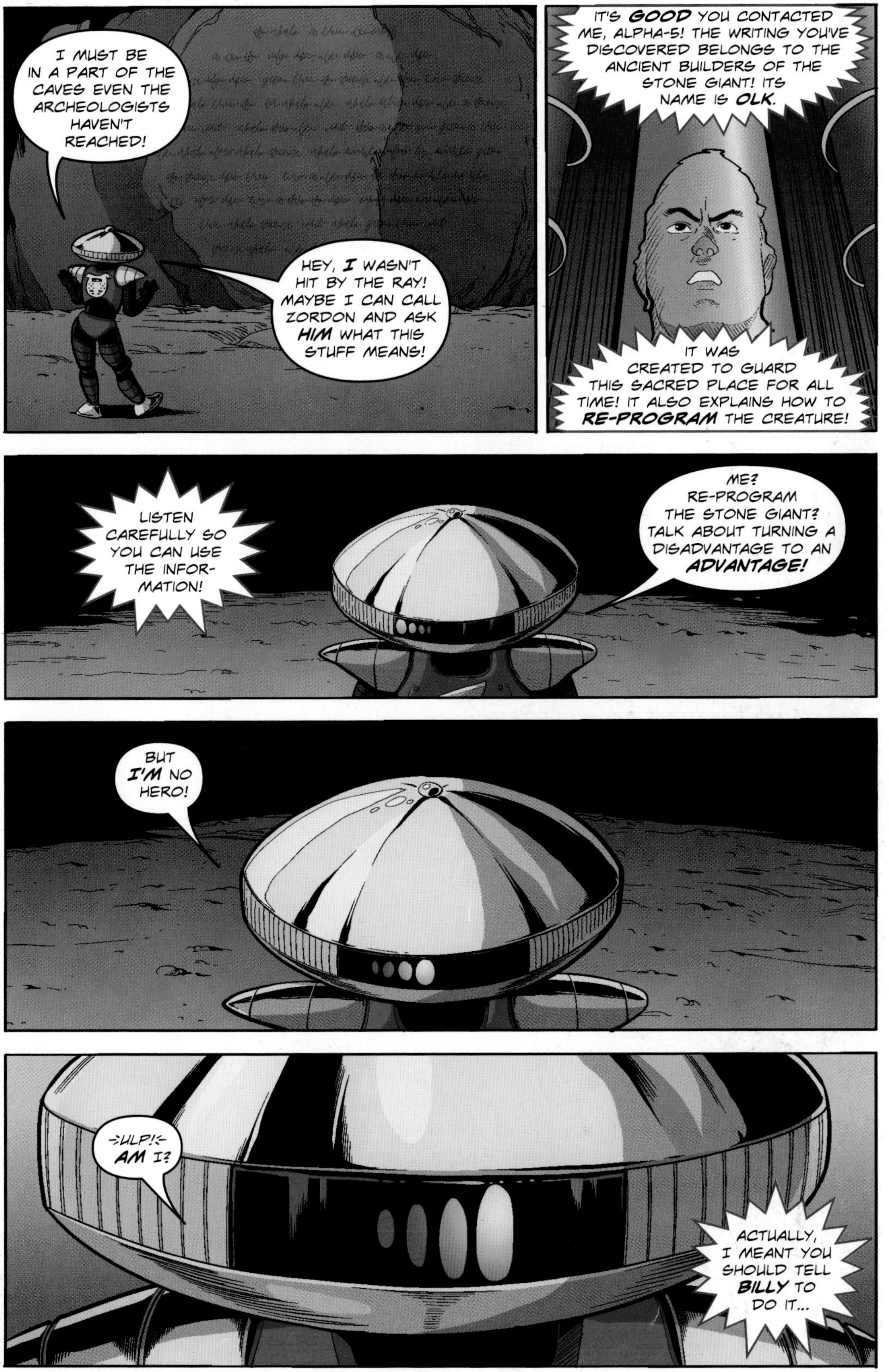
I MUST BE IN A PART OF THE CAVES EVEN THE ARCHEOLOGISTS HAVEN'T REACHED!
HEY, I WASN'T HIT BY THE RAY! MAYBE I CAN CALL ZORDON AND ASK HIM WHAT THIS STUFF MEANS!
IT'S GOOD YOU CONTACTED ME, ALPHA-5! THE WRITING YOU'VE DISCOVERED BELONGS TO THE ANCIENT BUILDERS OF THE STONE GIANT! ITS NAME IS OLK.
IT WAS CREATED TO GUARD THIS SACRED PLACE FOR ALL TIME! IT ALSO EXPLAINS HOW TO RE-PROGRAM THE CREATURE!
LISTEN CAREFULLY SO YOU CAN USE THE INFOR-MATION!
ME? RE-PROGRAM THE STONE GIANT? TALK ABOUT TURNING A DISADVANTAGE TO AN ADVANTAGE!
BUT I'M NO HERO!
=ULP!= AM I?
ACTUALLY, I MEANT YOU SHOULD TELL BILLY TO DO IT...

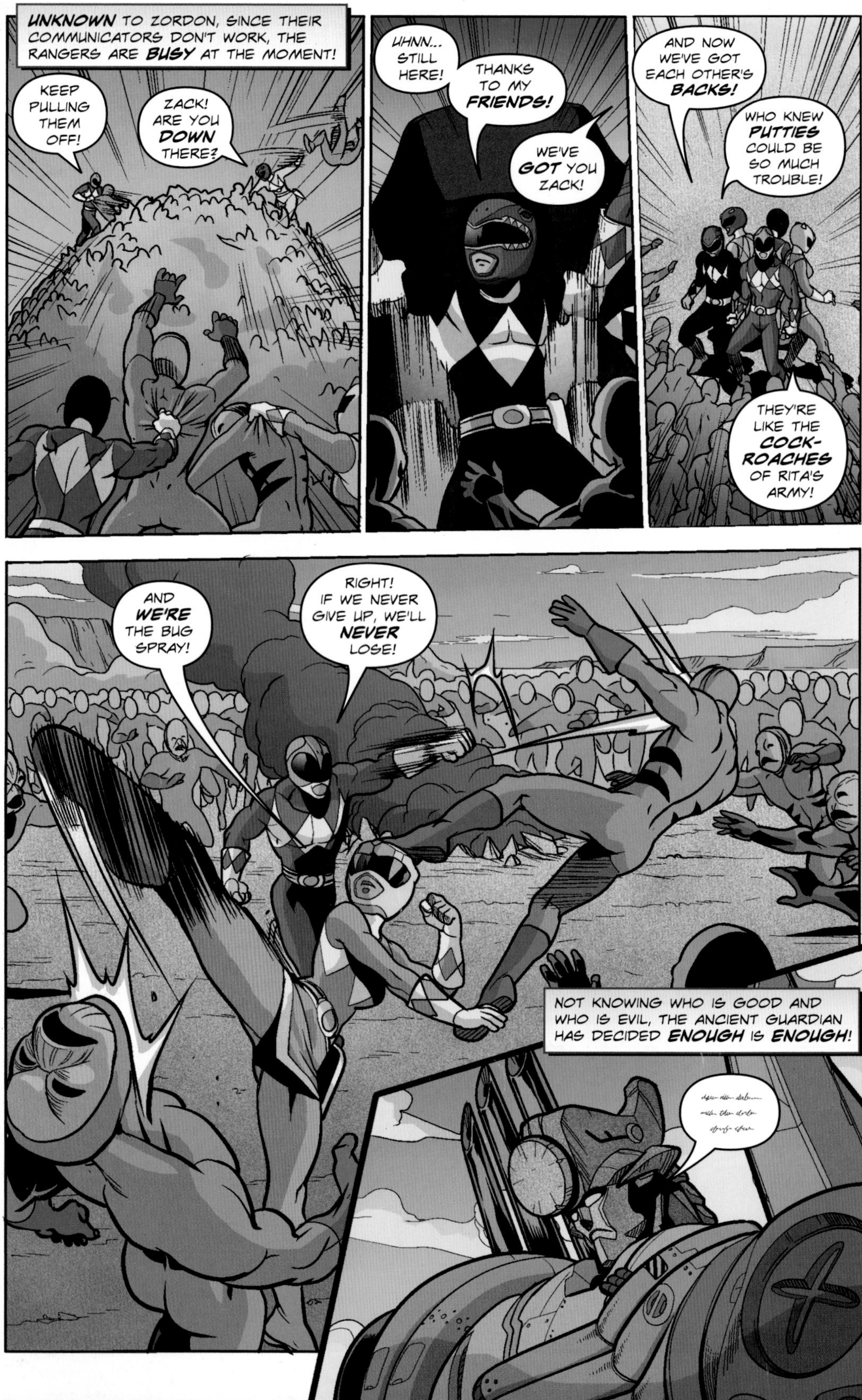
UNKNOWN TO ZORDON, SINCE THEIR COMMUNICATORS DON'T WORK, THE RANGERS ARE BUSY AT THE MOMENT!
KEEP PULLING THEM OFF!
ZACK! ARE YOU DOWN THERE?
UHNN... STILL HERE!
THANKS TO MY FRIENDS!
WE'VE GOT YOU ZACK!
AND NOW WE'VE GOT EACH OTHER'S BACKS!
WHO KNEW PUTTIES COULD BE SO MUCH TROUBLE!
THEY'RE LIKE THE COCK-ROACHES OF RITA'S ARMY!
AND WE'RE THE BUG SPRAY!
RIGHT! IF WE NEVER GIVE UP, WE'LL NEVER LOSE!
NOT KNOWING WHO IS GOOD AND WHO IS EVIL, THE ANCIENT GUARDIAN HAS DECIDED ENOUGH IS ENOUGH!

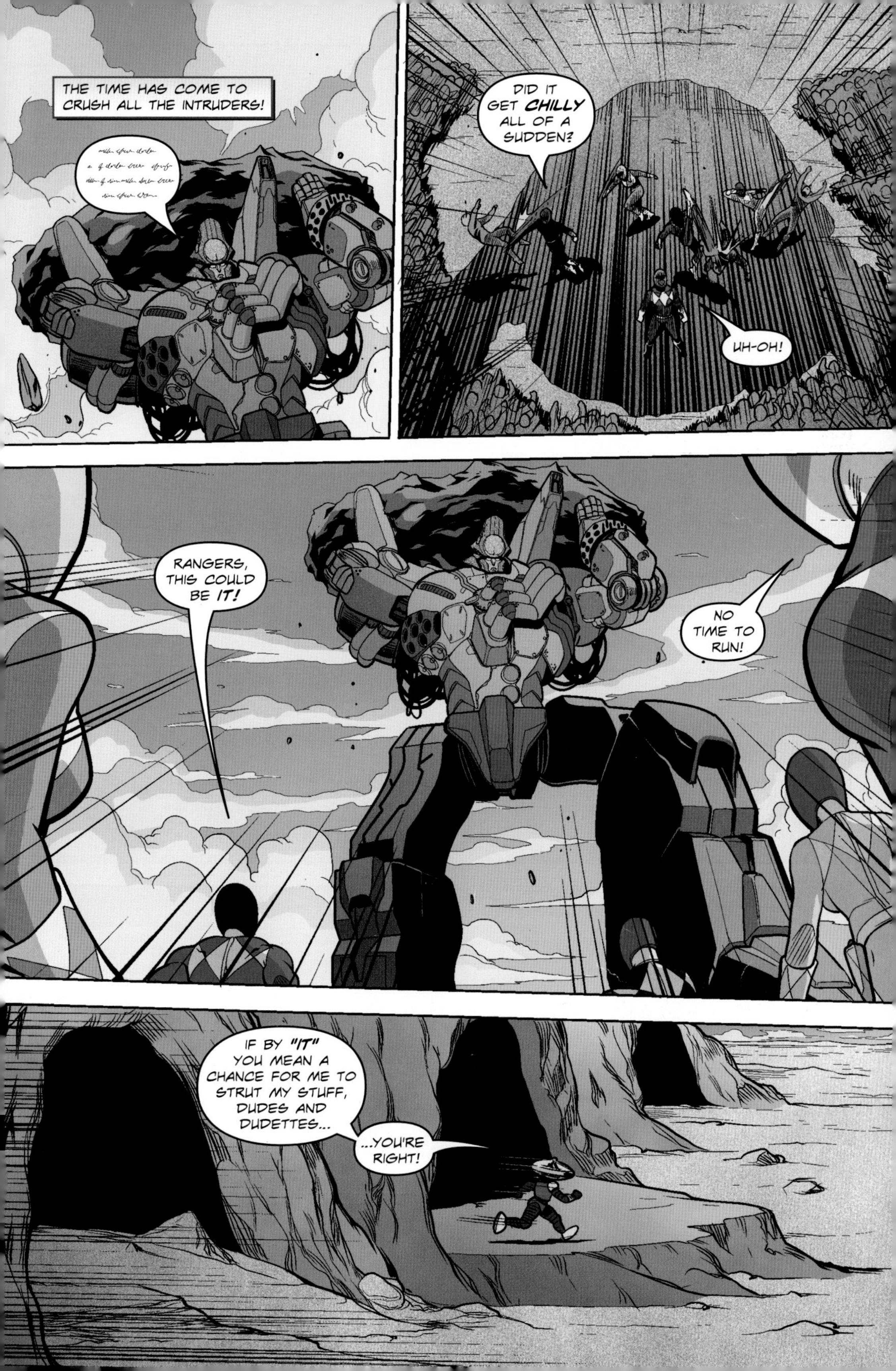
THE TIME HAS COME TO CRUSH ALL THE INTRUDERS!
DID IT GET CHILLY ALL OF A SUDDEN?
UH-OH!
RANGERS, THIS COULD BE IT!
NO TIME TO RUN!
IF BY "IT" YOU MEAN A CHANCE FOR ME TO STRUT MY STUFF, DUDES AND DUDETTES...
...YOU'RE RIGHT!

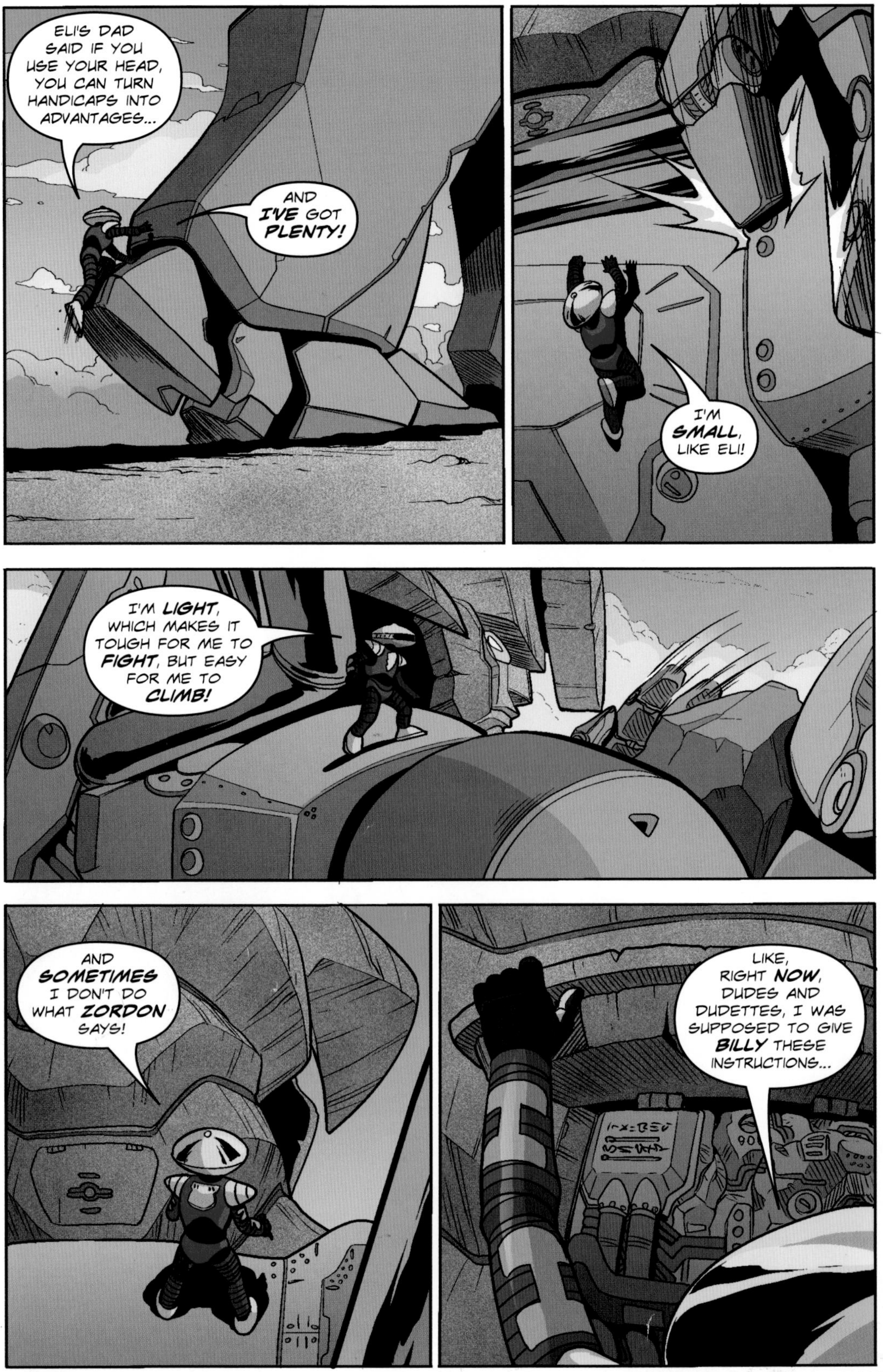
ELI'S DAD SAID IF YOU USE YOUR HEAD, YOU CAN TURN HANDICAPS INTO ADVANTAGES...
AND I'VE GOT PLENTY!
I'M SMALL, LIKE ELI!
I'M LIGHT, WHICH MAKES IT TOUGH FOR ME TO FIGHT, BUT EASY FOR ME TO CLIMB!
AND SOMETIMES I DON'T DO WHAT ZORDON SAYS!
LIKE, RIGHT NOW, DUDES AND DUDETTES, I WAS SUPPOSED TO GIVE BILLY THESE INSTRUCTIONS...

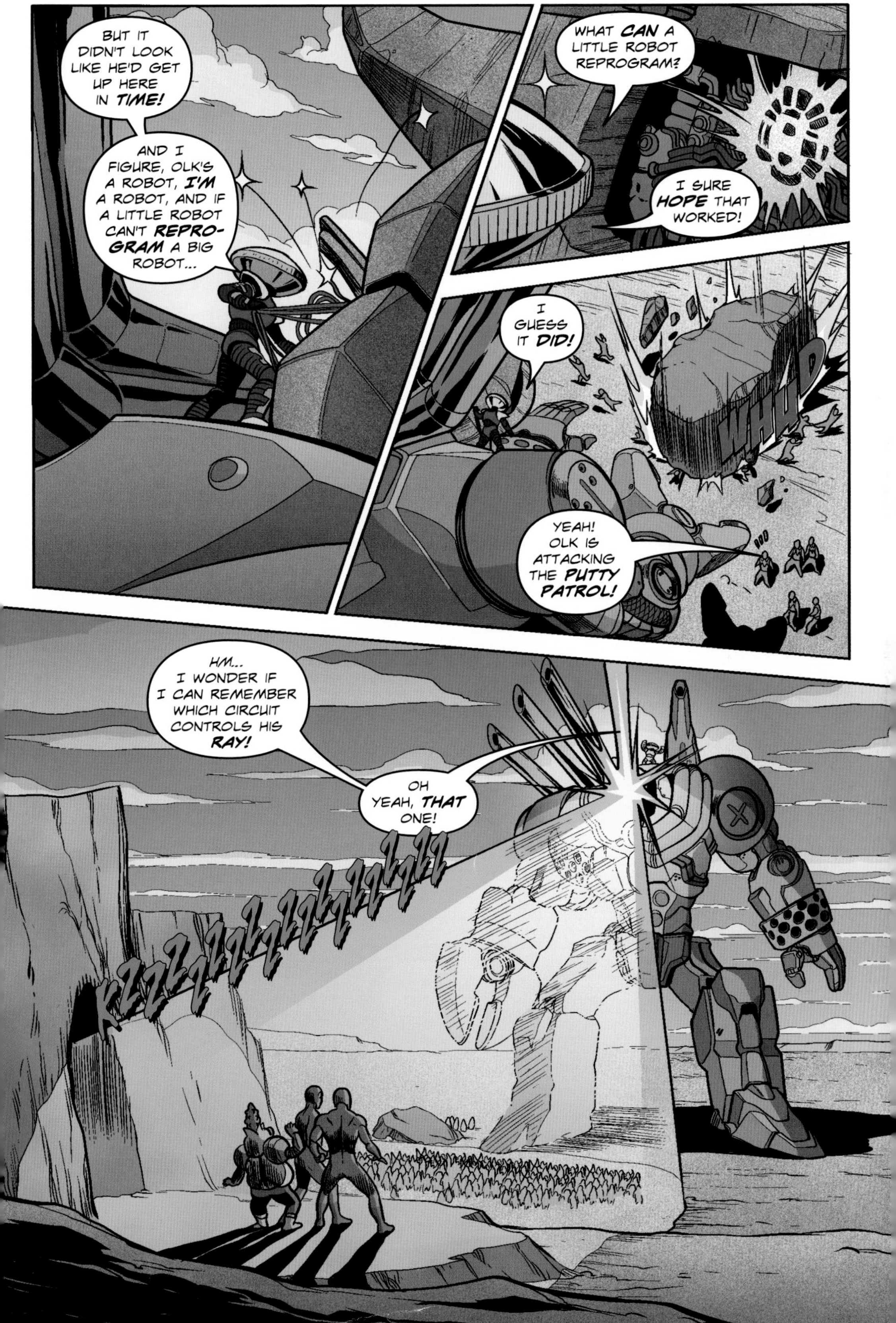
BUT IT DIDN'T LOOK LIKE HE'D GET UP HERE IN TIME!
AND I FIGURE, OLK'S A ROBOT, I'M A ROBOT, AND IF A LITTLE ROBOT CAN'T REPROGRAM A BIG ROBOT...
WHAT CAN A LITTLE ROBOT REPROGRAM?
I SURE HOPE THAT WORKED!
I GUESS IT DID!
WHUD
YEAH! OLK IS ATTACKING THE PUTTY PATROL!
HM... I WONDER IF I CAN REMEMBER WHICH CIRCUIT CONTROLS HIS RAY!
OH YEAH, THAT ONE!
KZZZZZZZZZZZZZZZZZZZ

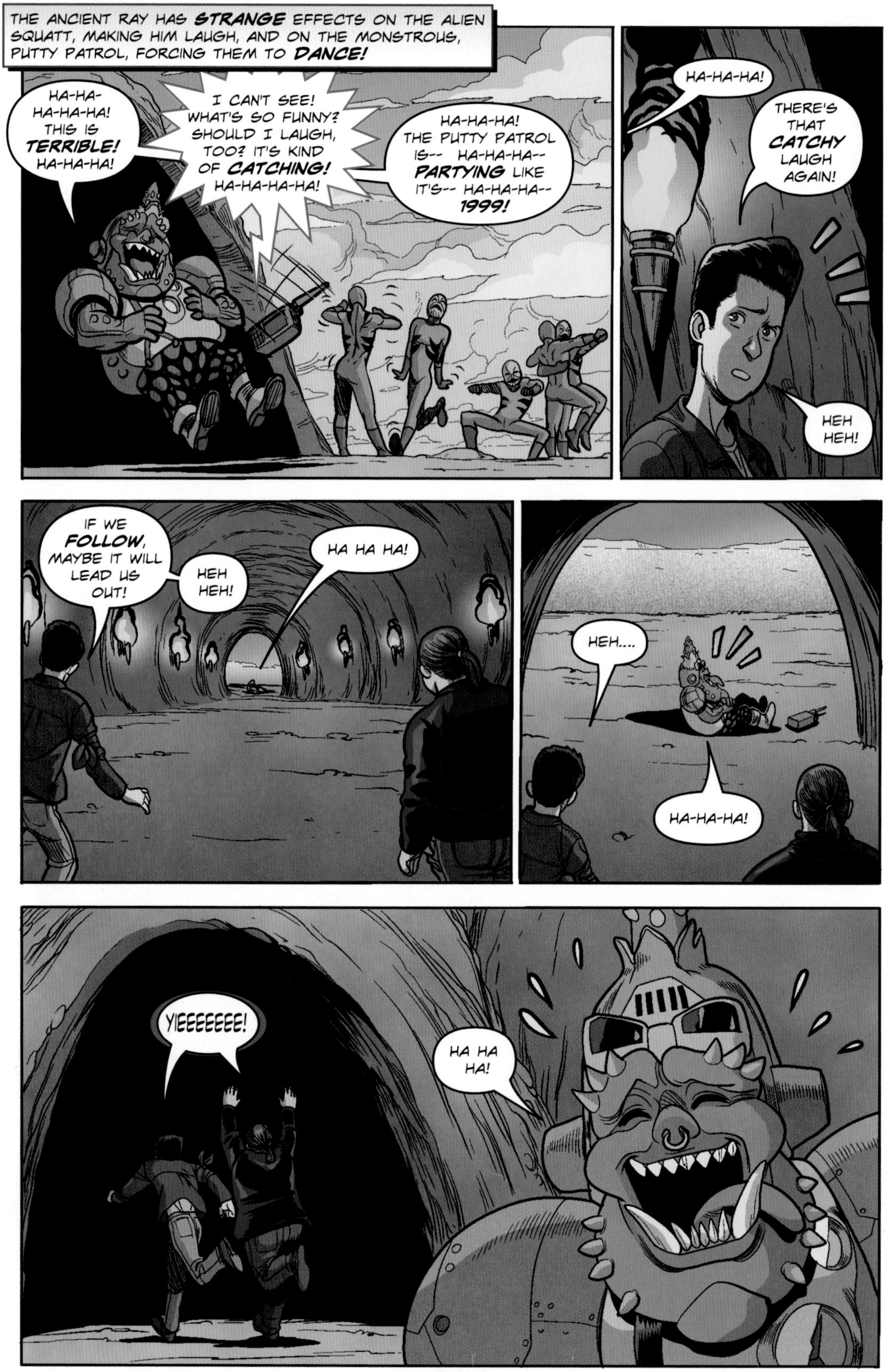
THE ANCIENT RAY HAS STRANGE EFFECTS ON THE ALIEN SQUATT, MAKING HIM LAUGH, AND ON THE MONSTROUS, PUTTY PATROL, FORCING THEM TO DANCE!
HA-HA-HA-HA-HA! THIS IS TERRIBLE! HA-HA-HA!
I CAN'T SEE! WHAT'S SO FUNNY? SHOULD I LAUGH, TOO? IT'S KIND OF CATCHING! HA-HA-HA-HA!
HA-HA-HA! THE PUTTY PATROL IS-- HA-HA-HA-- PARTYING LIKE IT'S-- HA-HA-HA-- 1999!
HA-HA-HA!
THERE'S THAT CATCHY LAUGH AGAIN!
HEH HEH!
IF WE FOLLOW, MAYBE IT WILL LEAD US OUT!
HEH HEH!
HA HA HA!
HEH....
HA-HA-HA!
YIEEEEEEE!
HA HA HA!

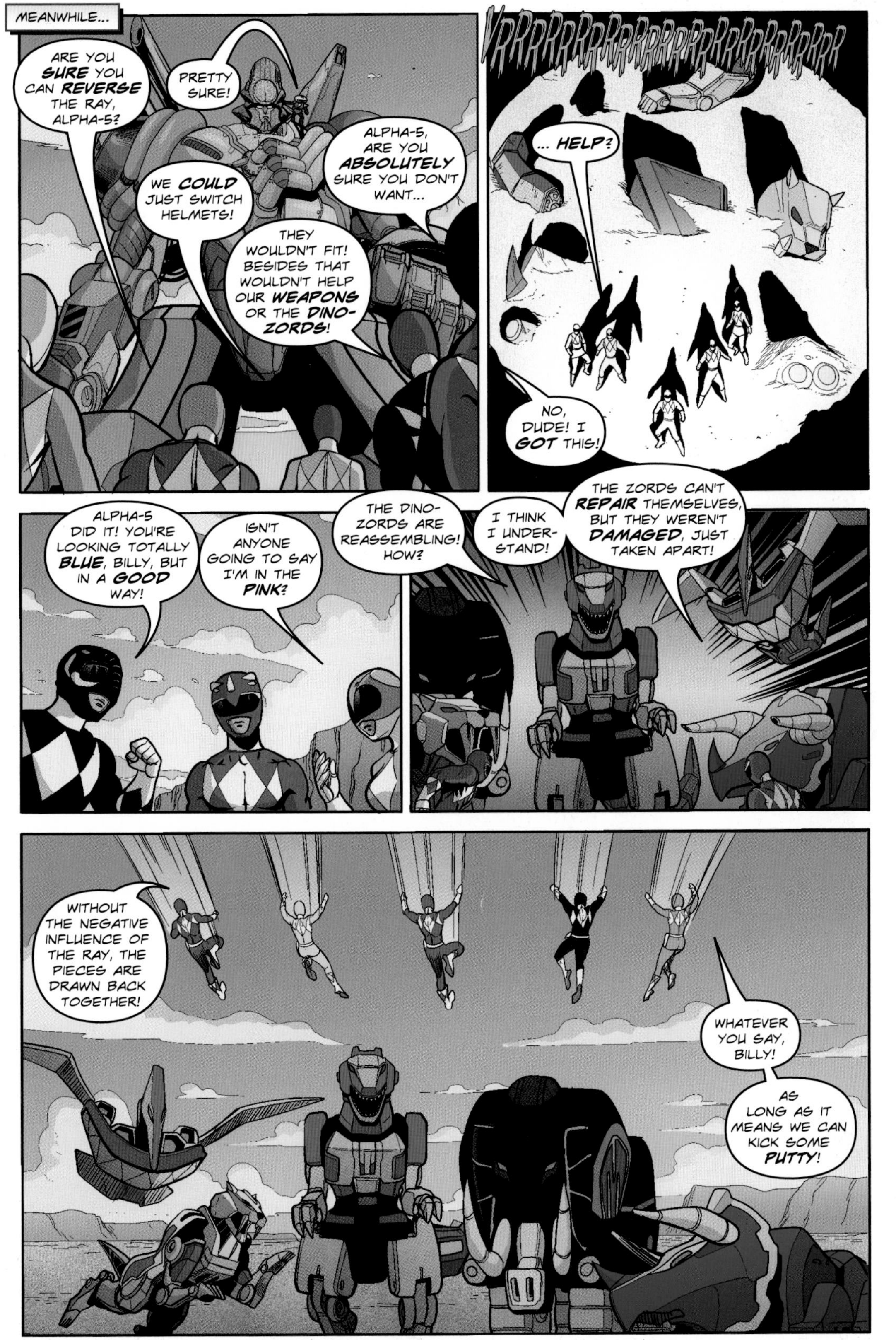
MEANWHILE...
ARE YOU SURE YOU CAN REVERSE THE RAY, ALPHA-5?
PRETTY SURE!
WE COULD JUST SWITCH HELMETS!
ALPHA-5, ARE YOU ABSOLUTELY SURE YOU DON'T WANT...
THEY WOULDN'T FIT! BESIDES THAT WOULDN'T HELP OUR WEAPONS OR THE DINO-ZORDS!
VRRRRRRRRRRRRRRRRRRRRRRRRRRRRR
... HELP?
NO, DUDE! I GOT THIS!
ALPHA-5 DID IT! YOU'RE LOOKING TOTALLY BLUE, BILLY, BUT IN A GOOD WAY!
ISN'T ANYONE GOING TO SAY I'M IN THE PINK?
THE DINO-ZORDS ARE REASSEMBLING! HOW?
I THINK I UNDER-STAND!
THE ZORDS CAN'T REPAIR THEMSELVES, BUT THEY WEREN'T DAMAGED, JUST TAKEN APART!
WITHOUT THE NEGATIVE INFLUENCE OF THE RAY, THE PIECES ARE DRAWN BACK TOGETHER!
WHATEVER YOU SAY, BILLY!
AS LONG AS IT MEANS WE CAN KICK SOME PUTTY!

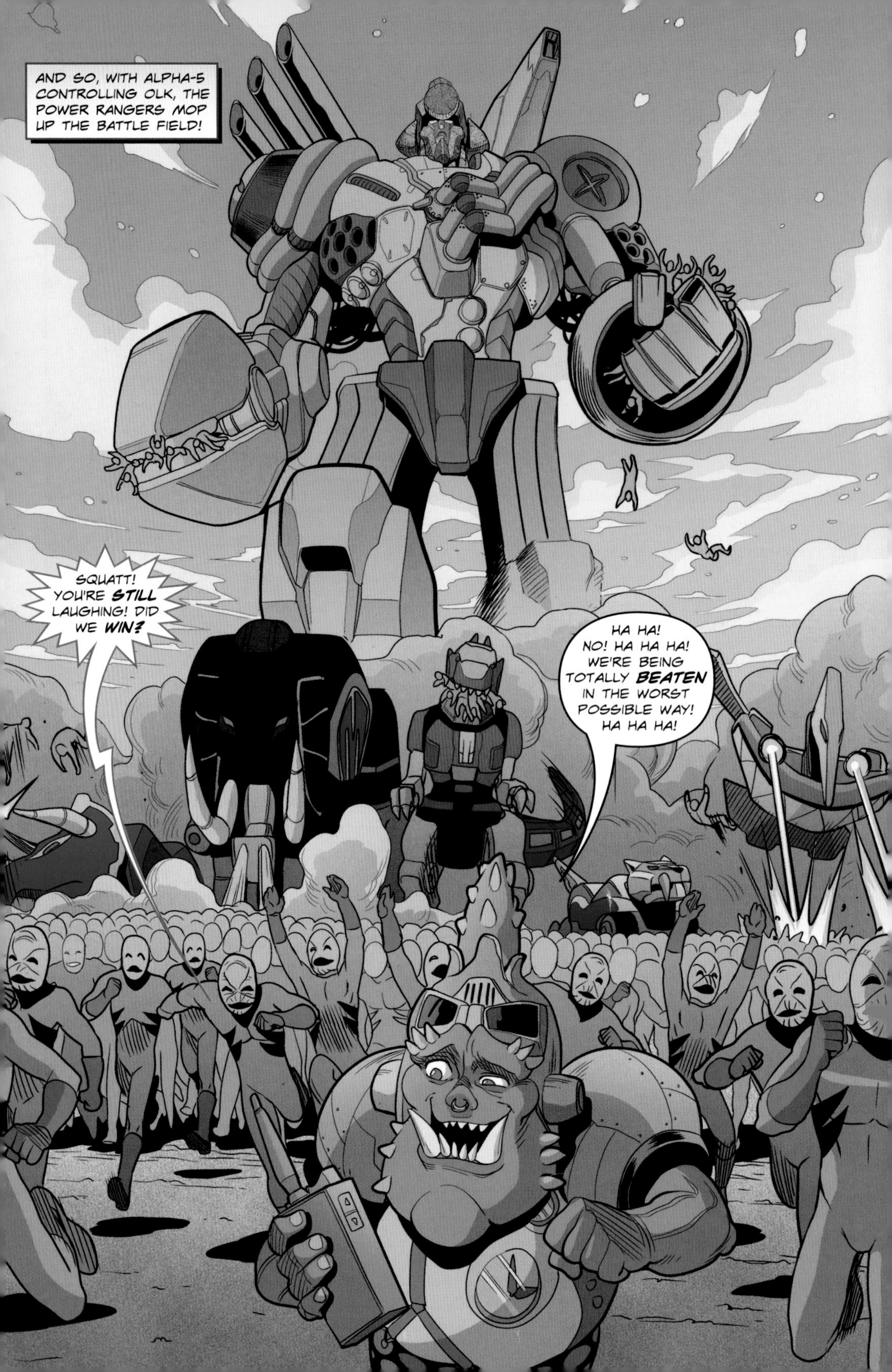
AND SO, WITH ALPHA-5 CONTROLLING OLK, THE POWER RANGERS MOP UP THE BATTLE FIELD!
SQUATT! YOU'RE STILL LAUGHING! DID WE WIN?
HA HA! NO! HA HA HA! WE'RE BEING TOTALLY BEATEN IN THE WORST POSSIBLE WAY! HA HA HA!

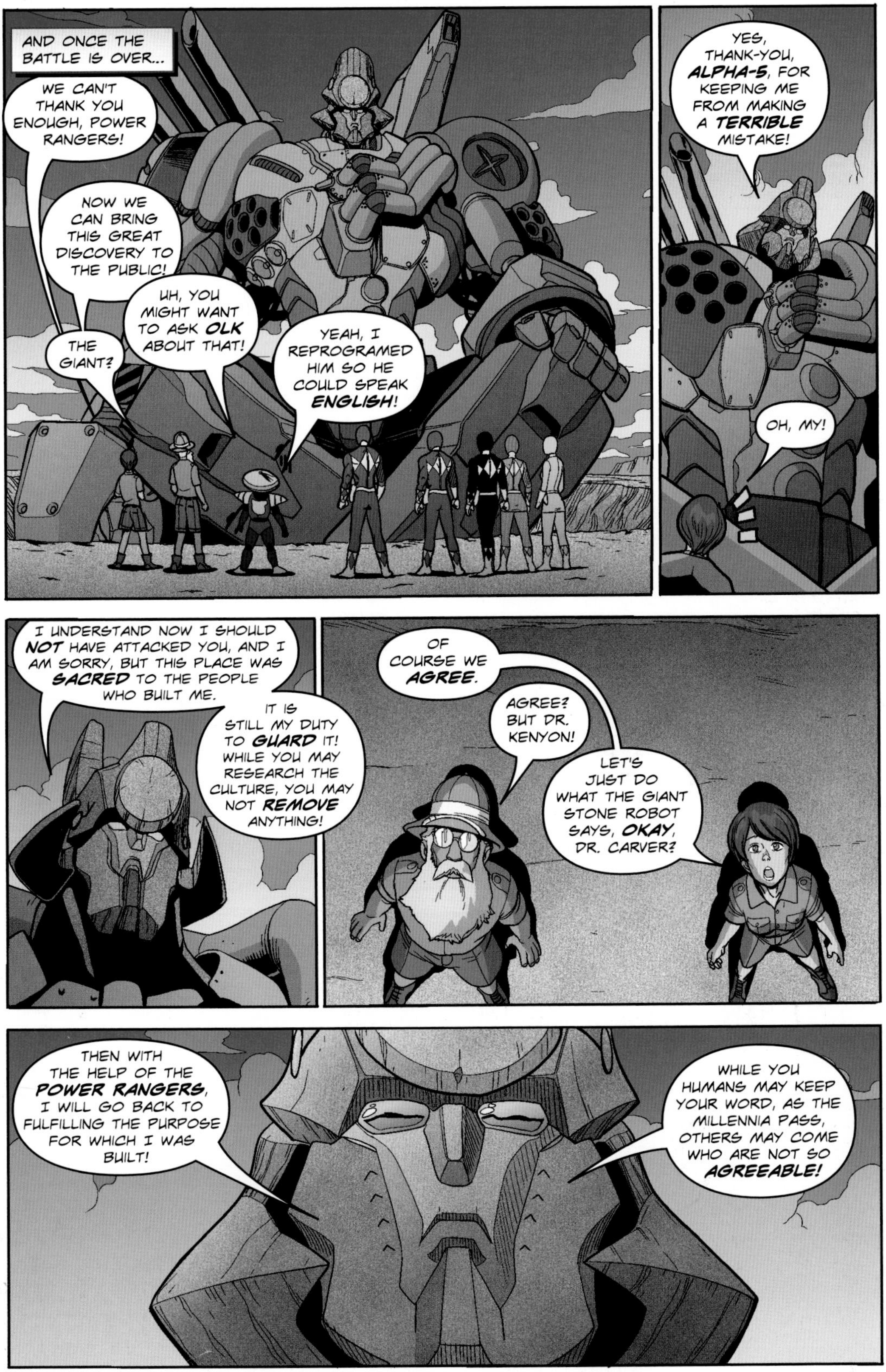
AND ONCE THE BATTLE IS OVER...
WE CAN'T THANK YOU ENOUGH, POWER RANGERS!
NOW WE CAN BRING THIS GREAT DISCOVERY TO THE PUBLIC!
THE GIANT?
UH, YOU MIGHT WANT TO ASK OLK ABOUT THAT!
YEAH, I REPROGRAMED HIM SO HE COULD SPEAK ENGLISH!
YES, THANK-YOU, ALPHA-5, FOR KEEPING ME FROM MAKING A TERRIBLE MISTAKE!
OH, MY!
I UNDERSTAND NOW I SHOULD NOT HAVE ATTACKED YOU, AND I AM SORRY, BUT THIS PLACE WAS SACRED TO THE PEOPLE WHO BUILT ME.
IT IS STILL MY DUTY TO GUARD IT! WHILE YOU MAY RESEARCH THE CULTURE, YOU MAY NOT REMOVE ANYTHING!
OF COURSE WE AGREE.
AGREE? BUT DR. KENYON!
LET'S JUST DO WHAT THE GIANT STONE ROBOT SAYS, OKAY, DR. CARVER?
THEN WITH THE HELP OF THE POWER RANGERS, I WILL GO BACK TO FULFILLING THE PURPOSE FOR WHICH I WAS BUILT!
WHILE YOU HUMANS MAY KEEP YOUR WORD, AS THE MILLENNIA PASS, OTHERS MAY COME WHO ARE NOT SO AGREEABLE!

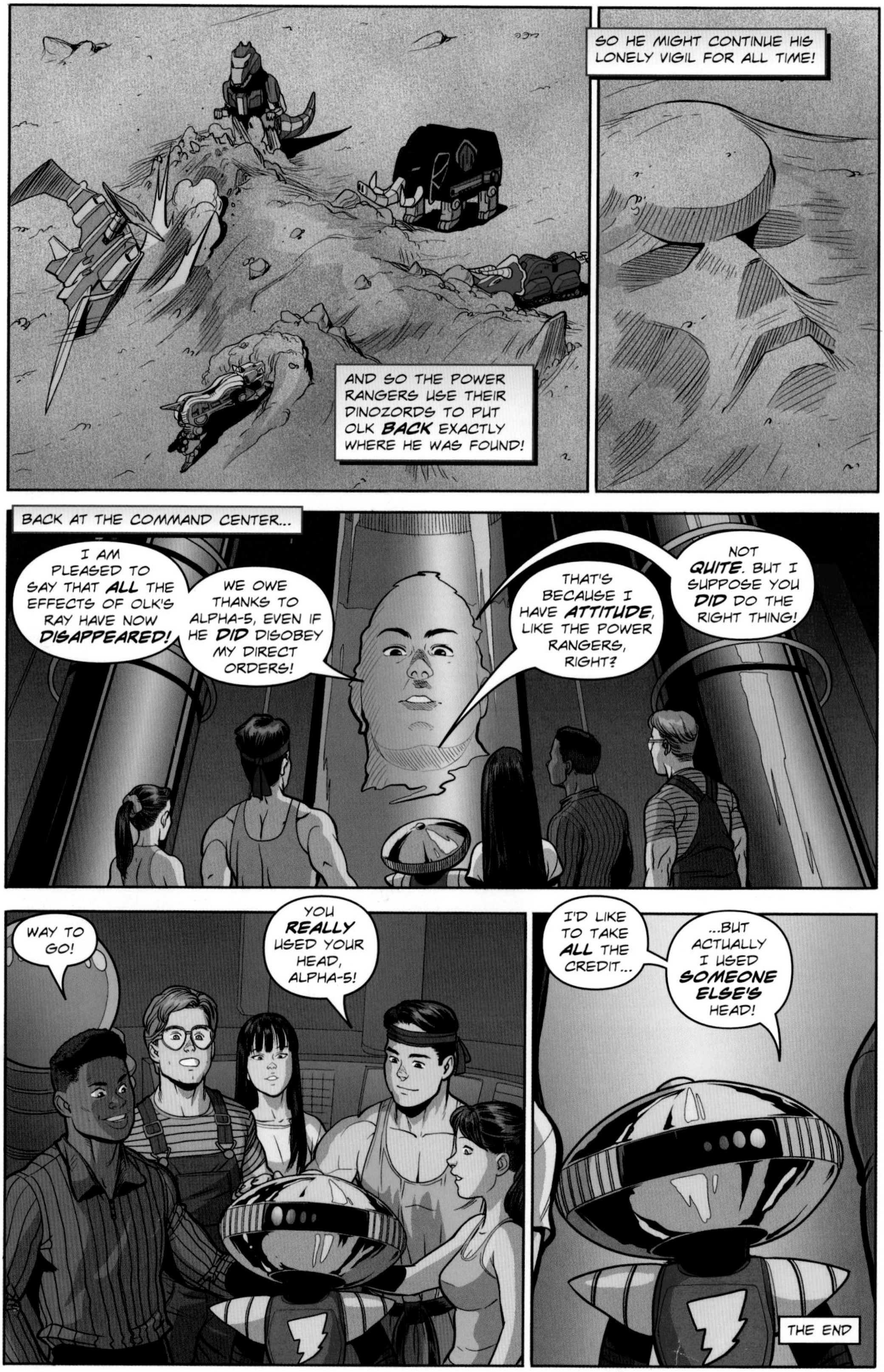
AND SO THE POWER RANGERS USE THEIR DINOZORDS TO PUT OLK BACK EXACTLY WHERE HE WAS FOUND!
SO HE MIGHT CONTINUE HIS LONELY VIGIL FOR ALL TIME!
BACK AT THE COMMAND CENTER...
I AM PLEASED TO SAY THAT ALL THE EFFECTS OF OLK'S RAY HAVE NOW DISAPPEARED!
WE OWE THANKS TO ALPHA-5, EVEN IF HE DID DISOBEY MY DIRECT ORDERS!
THAT'S BECAUSE I HAVE ATTITUDE, LIKE THE POWER RANGERS, RIGHT?
NOT QUITE. BUT I SUPPOSE YOU DID DO THE RIGHT THING!
WAY TO GO!
YOU REALLY USED YOUR HEAD, ALPHA-5!
I'D LIKE TO TAKE ALL THE CREDIT...
...BUT ACTUALLY I USED SOMEONE ELSE'S HEAD!
THE END

WATCH OUT FOR PAPERCUTZ™

Welcome to the first MIGHTY MORPHIN POWER RANGERS graphic novel, by Stefan Petrucha and PH Marcondes, from Papercutz, the perpetually-morphing comics company dedicated to publishing great graphic novels for all ages. I'm Jim Salicrup, the Editor-in-Chief, and I'm here to take you behind-the-scenes to explain exactly how this graphic novel came to be.

But first, I have to go into my rant. Once upon a time, comics (there really weren't any "graphic novels" back then) in North America were essentially for everyone. While generally considered kids' stuff, anyone could and would enjoy comics, no matter how old they were, or whether they were male or female. There was a comicbook for him or her. Now, things are a little different. Many comics and graphic novels are created for adults. Some, of course, are created just for children. But, if a comic or graphic novel declares itself suitable for all ages—well, folks think that just means kids. Which brings us to the MIGHTY MORPHIN POWER RANGERS.

FREE COMIC BOOK DAY
ALL-NEW!
MIGHTY MORPHIN
POWER RANGERS
PAPERCUTZ

Clearly, the original *Mighty Morphin Power Rangers* TV series was created for children. But those children who were fans of the original series are now adults, and many are into comics and graphic novels. When Papercutz first announced that we were launching a new series of POWER RANGERS graphic novels, the one question I got repeatedly was, "Which Power Rangers?" As PR fans all know, there have many incarnations of the Power Rangers over the past twenty years, the show keeps morphin into new series for new generations of fans. And whenever I answered an adult fan, and said we were publishing POWER RANGERS SUPER SAMURAI, they seemed to instantly lose interest, because that wasn't "their" Power Rangers. Always eager to please, I had to ask who were their Power Rangers, and the answer came back loud and clear—the MIGHTY MORPHIN POWER RANGERS! Countless fans would ask, and often demand, that we bring them back. And obviously, we did just that.

But as an Editor-in-Chief of a comics company, one of the things you wind up doing a lot is worry. In general, one of the biggest worries (and heartbreaks) is the fear of producing a wonderful graphic novel, with brilliant writing and awesome artwork, and no one finds out about it. And that was my concern with MIGHTY MORPHIN POWER RANGERS. Turns out, when we announced that we were bringing back MMPR at the San Diego Comic-Con, people paid attention! The Internet was suddenly all abuzz about the return of these classic super-heroes! Yet as we get closer and closer to our publication date, I'm still worried.

I'm worried that the fans that are most interested in this graphic novel, won't find us. If you're one of those fans, and you found us, I can't tell you how happy I am! I'm worried that this graphic novel will be shelved in the Children's Books sections in bookstores and the Kids Comics section in comicbook shops. Now, many people can't understand why that would worry me, after all, isn't MIGHTY MORPHIN POWER RANGERS a children's show? Well, yeah, over twenty years ago! Unless the original fans now have children of their own, how will they find us? One way we hope to direct comics fans to MIGHTY MORPHIN POWER RANGERS is by publishing a Free Comic Book Day comic featuring an all-new story, by our stellar creative team of Petrucha and Marcondes. (If you missed that, don't worry—we'll be collecting that story soon in an upcoming graphic novel!) Another way to bring attention to this series will be bringing on best-selling author, star of the TV series *Paranormal State*, and major MMPR fan Ryan Buell to co-write the next graphic novel along with Stefan.

Will it all work? Will the Mighty Morphin Power Ranger fans find us and enjoy what Stefan and PH (not to mention colorist, Laurie E. Smith, letterer, Bryan Senka, and Editor, Michael Petranek) created here? You tell us! Contact us through the means listed below, and let us know what you think! After all, if you didn't tell us you wanted the MIGHTY MORPHIN POWER RANGERS, this graphic novel simply wouldn't exist!

Go, go, POWER RANGERS!

Thanks,

Jim

STAY IN TOUCH!

EMAIL:	salicrup@papercutz.com
WEB:	www.papercutz.com
TWITTER:	@papercutzgn
FACEBOOK:	PAPERCUTZGRAPHICNOVELS
SNAIL MAIL:	Papercutz, 160 Broadway, Suite 700, East Wing,New York, NY 10038

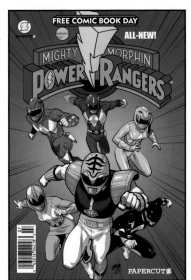

Mighty Morphin

A LOOK

It's Morphin Time!

Twenty years ago, an intergalactic being named Zordon ordered his friend and assistant, Alpha 5, to teleport five overbearing and overemotional humans (i.e. teenagers) to the Power Rangers Command Center and begin their journey as the first Power Rangers. August 28, 1993 marked an important date in television history with the first airing of *Mighty Morphin Power Rangers* on FOX. The show rapidly reached the hearts of children and became one of the most popular live-action

Rita Repulsa and her crew in "Day of the Dumpster," the first episode of "Mighty Morphin Power Rangers"

kid's series in the past two decades, with over 700 Power Rangers TV episodes having aired. The demographic spread from North America to more than 150 countries around the world with international airings of the shows, a live tour, two feature films (*Mighty Morphin Power Rangers: The Movie* and *Turbo: A Power Rangers Movie*), and countless products from a variety of licensees ranging from toys, video games, books, clothing, and household goods. The Power Rangers franchise was originally owned by Saban, bought by Disney, and then re-acquired by Saban Brands a few years ago.

Mighty Morphin Power Rangers was the beginning of a long line of Power Rangers. Each season followed the same concept of five chosen, good-hearted humans defending the planet Earth. The teenagers represent different cultures and nationalities but work together for the greater good. The original season taught great values to children through episodes and public service announcements.

Children and teenagers who watched the show in the first season are now adults who watch the show with their kids. I still remember watching the first episode, "Day of the Dumpster" with my little brother. We watched the episodes repeatedly and collected all of the toys. Now, I spread the love of the show with my two nephews (ages 2 and 6) and my kids (ages 1 and 3). Every time that I visit my nephews, they are running around the house with their Power Rangers Megaforce toys and cards. My daughter dressed as the Pink Megaforce Ranger for Halloween with great pride. I grew up watching Power Rangers while facing typical challenges in junior high school and high school. The show has always been a positive effect in my life and a major reason for becoming an active member in the online Power Rangers community.

Power Rangers is targeted for a young audience but has an extensive fanbase that spans to teenagers and adults. The

Power Rangers: BACK

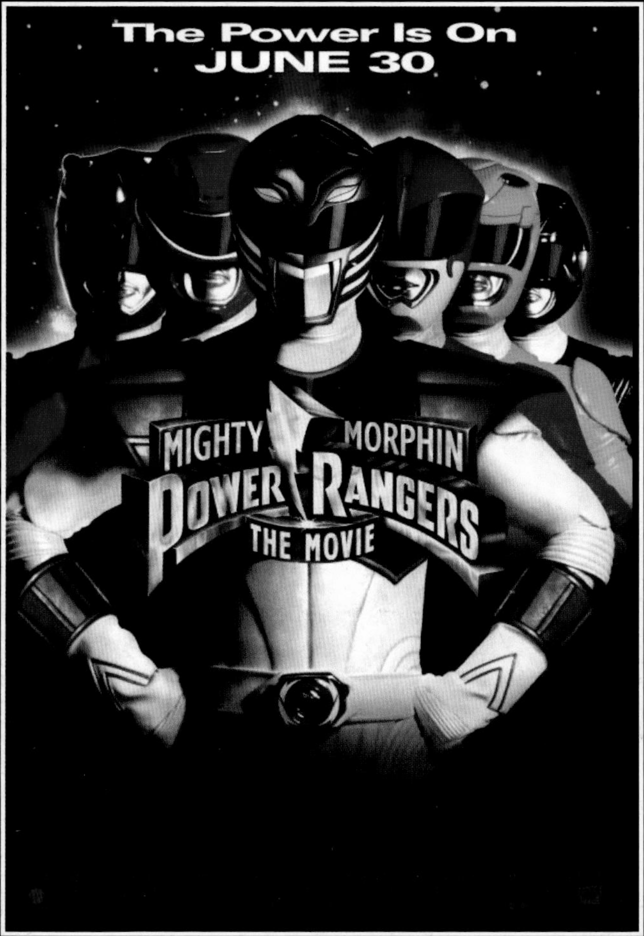

The Power Is On
JUNE 30
MIGHTY MORPHIN
POWER RANGERS
THE MOVIE

Movie Poster for "Mighty Morphin Power Rangers The Movie"

After Saban Brands re-purchased the Power Rangers brand, the Power Rangers name expanded with an official Twitter, Facebook, and Instagram.

Over 20 years after its debut, fans can watch every single episode of Power Rangers on Netflix. Shout!-Factory recently released the Power Rangers Legacy Collection, which has twenty years of Power Rangers episodes in a single DVD Set. Bandai America has released Power Rangers Action Card Game and Ranger Keys, featuring Rangers from the past 20 years. Bandai has also tailored to the collectors with the Power Rangers 20th Anniversary Legacy toyline. Mega Bloks released the Mighty Morphin Power Rangers 20th anniversary collector pack in late 2013.

The anniversary celebration continues with the 2014 Power Rangers Super Megaforce season. The Power Rangers will utilize their new Legendary Morphers and Ranger Keys to unlock the Powers of past Rangers. New and old fans will be able to watch twenty years of history as the Super Megaforce Rangers harness past weapons, Zords, and Megazords in addition to an explosive season finale with special Power Rangers guests. After 21 years, it appears that the Power Rangers franchise is just getting started!

first official Power Rangers convention took place in 2007 with two more following in 2010 and 2012. These conventions allow fans to interact with fellow fans and cast/crew members from the show. The Power Rangers online fandom has existed since the show began. Fans from all over the world are able to discuss the show and share their contributions through sites, blogs, and forums.

-Umesh Patel, Ranger Crew

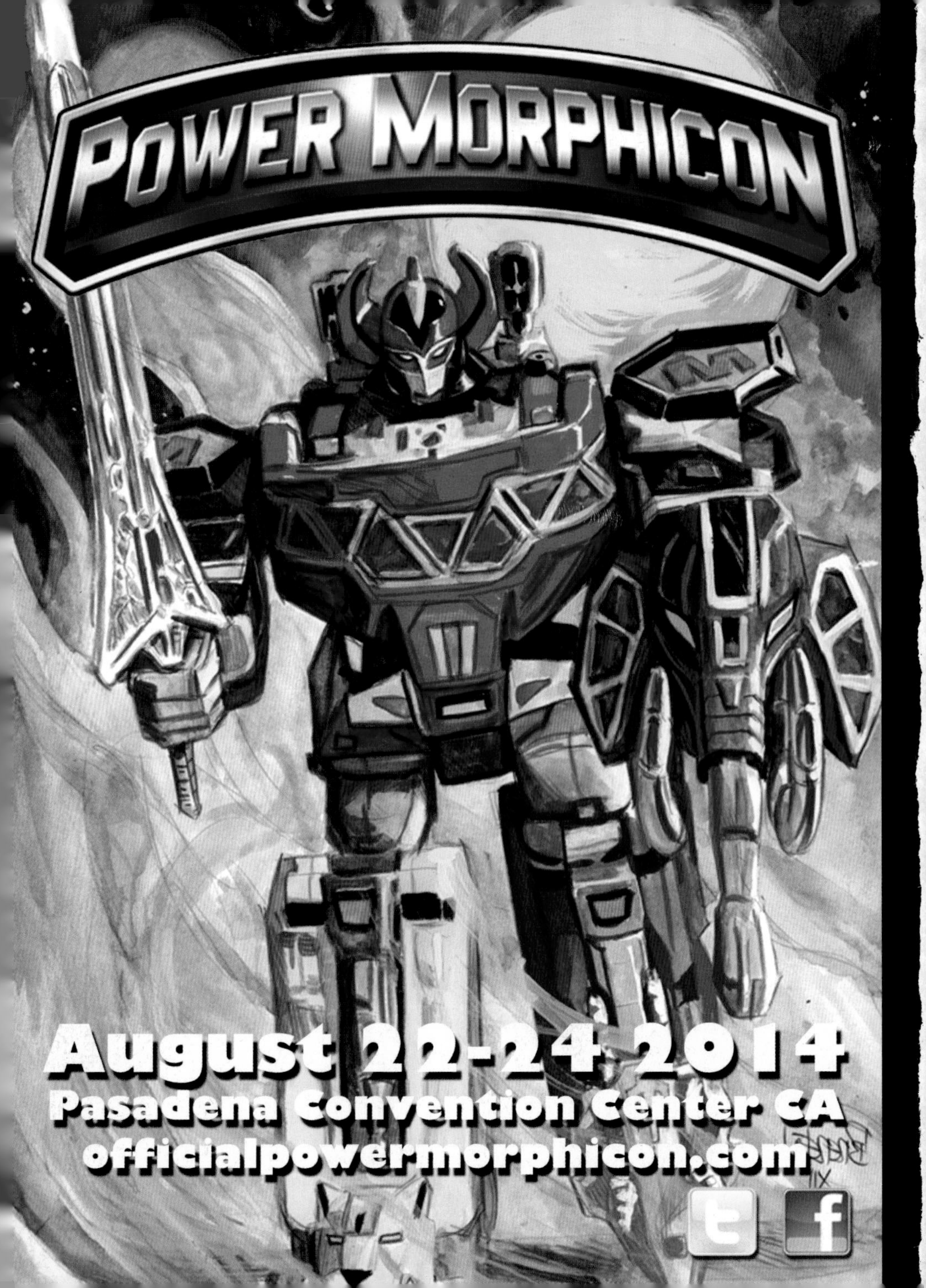
POWER MORPHICON
August 22-24 2014
Pasadena Convention Center CA
officialpowermorphicon.com

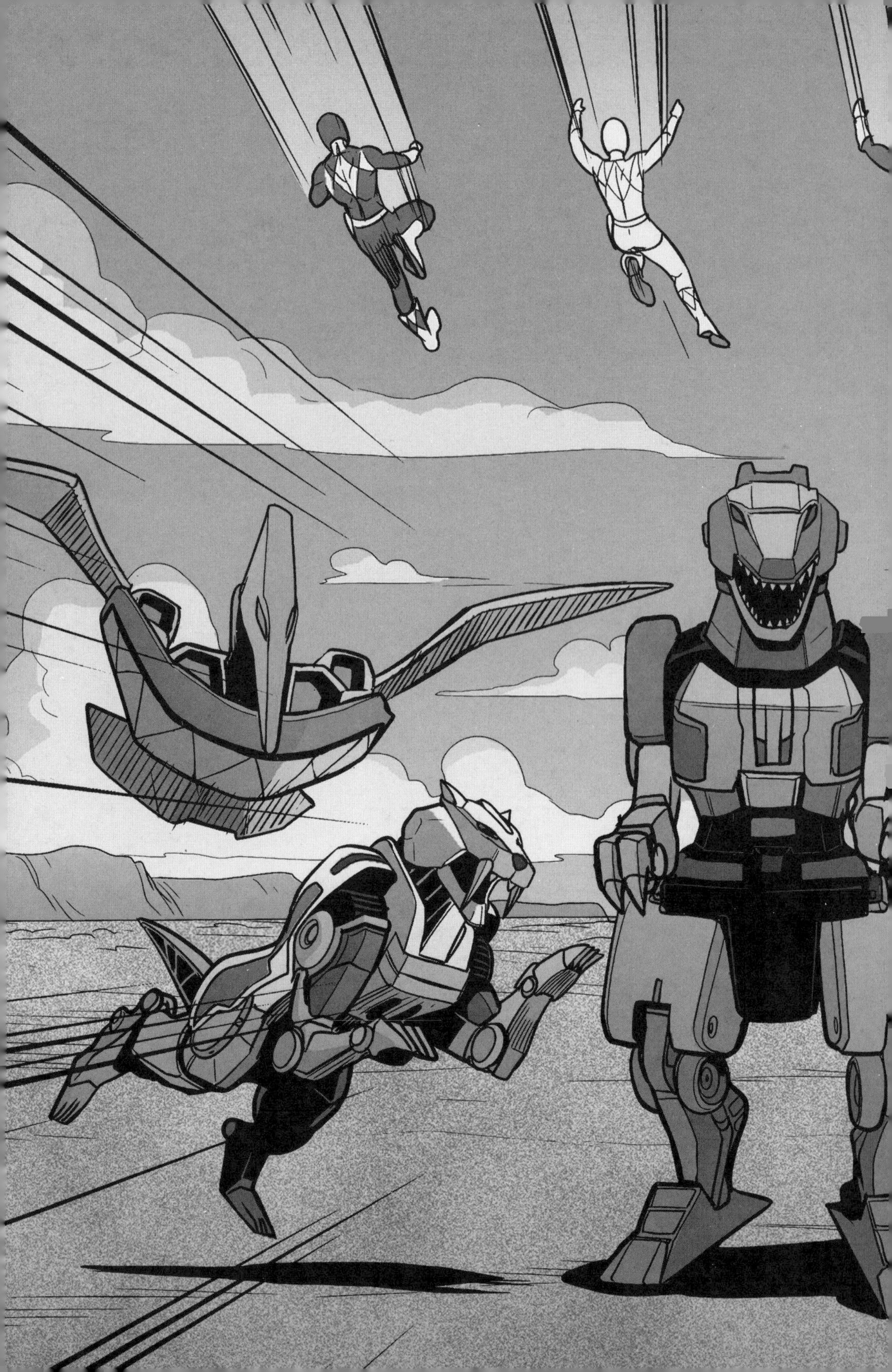